All My Sins Remembered

Ron Cooper

Goliad Press
McAllen, Texas

Published by Goliad Press
McAllen, Texas

First Edition

Acknowledgements:

I am deeply grateful to the College of Central Florida for awarding
me a sabbatical during which I researched this novel. I also thank
Tom Ziesemer and the Marion County Sheriff's Office for information
on law enforcement practices. Thanks, of course, to John Molina,
Eric Miles Williamson, Dan Mendoza, Kim Davis, Joe Haske, and
everyone associated with Goliad Press.

Book Design: Daniel Mendoza and Kim Davis

Printed in the United States of America

ISBN: 9781948428019

Library of Congress Control Number: 2018931118

www.goliadreview.com

All My Sins
Remembered

For Sandra, my world.

All My Sins
Remembered

FEBRUARY, 2018

The barrel of the .45 felt good in Blevins's mouth. The muzzle rested in the hollow of his palate, the front sight in the crease along his tongue. The first few times he had sucked the smooth steel the metallic taste was disheartening. A bloodlike flavor in the mouth as one's last sensation could ruin the whole event. Now, the taste was familiar, welcome and warm, like good bourbon. If he kept it in long enough, it would seem to soften, and he imagined he could leave his teeth marks in it, like in a pencil. He smiled at the notion of a revolver barrel as a writing implement.

Through the gap between the lines of trees along the far side of the Silver River, Blevins had a clear view of a pale yellow full moon. The silhouette of a slender bird, probably an egret, passed across it. What better final sight?

The dispatcher said something about a report of a dead body in the Forest. Blevins pressed the revolver's trigger, steadied the hammer with his thumb, and removed the barrel from his mouth. He wiped the spit from the muzzle on his shirt and holstered his sidearm as he slid down from the hood of the department vehicle. He got into the car, wedged the bottle of whiskey between his thighs, and picked up the radio.

"Maggie, it's Blevins. I'm out that way. What's the situation?"

"Got a call from a Starlight. They found a campsite and think the occupant is dead."

"I didn't even know they were back already. Usual location?"

"Yes. I'm surprised they even reported it."

"I'm on the way."

Blevins upended the bottle for a last swallow and stuffed it under the seat. He left the boat landing, pulled onto East State

Road 40 to head deeper into the Ocala National Forest, and wondered if answering the call was testimony to his dedication as a law enforcement officer or one more instance of weakness of will. He had already imagined the newspaper story. "Major Blevins Bombardi, a twenty-eight-year veteran of the Marion County Sheriff's Department, was found dead on the hood of his car. The cause of death is unknown." Perhaps just this once the paper would instead have the guts to tell the real story instead of displaying its usual timidity concerning suicide. "He died from a self-inflicted gun shot to the head. Blood was splattered over the windshield of the department vehicle. He was in uniform. The coroner found high levels of alcohol in Bombardi's blood. Bombardi is reported to have suffered from depression since the highly publicized death of his wife in 2016."

★ ★ ★ ★ ★ ★ ★ ★ ★ ★ ★ ★ ★ ★ ★

The western edge of the Ocala National Forest is three miles east of town and covers over 600 square miles of pine, scrub oak, hardwood hammocks, lakes, and rivers. Millions of tourists visit year-round to hike, camp, kayak, and try to catch glimpses of black bears, bobcats, and alligators. Wood-frame, four-room houses and mildewed mobile homes align the narrow roads, occupied by folks whom Ocala residents generally consider unsavory. When an Ocalan says that someone is from the Forest, the message is that the person is at best uncouth but probably a shiftless squatter on the run from the law. Truant young men are known as Forest Rats, whose idea of recreation is trolling for gators by means of a large treble hook baited with a live squirrel behind a jon boat and catching cooters, freshwater turtles, to shove hoses into their mouths and gorge them with water until the shells explode.

As a young deputy Blevins spent most of his days patrolling the Forest roads, occasionally arresting drug dealers and manufacturers and burglars who stole chainsaws and satellite dishes from each other to dump in the pawn shops, the primary entrepreneurial endeavor of the community of Silver Springs, a thin buffer between Ocala and the Forest.

The Forest is also home for a few weeks each February to the Starlight Family of Cosmic Energy, a band of several hundred young vagabonds who have rejected what they selectively deem society to follow the seasons around the country sleeping in decrepit pup tents and espousing universal love and some ill-articulated form of animism populated by nature and biochemical spirits. To local businesses, they are better known for smoking marijuana and eating psilocybin mushrooms in addition to pilfering their necessities from those businesses. They are seen hitchhiking between the Forest and Ocala in threes and fours in their hemp shirts and sandals made from blown out tires and a few inches of rope.

Blevins turned onto the macadam road that led to where the Starlights set up camp each year. The road was flanked on both sides by a variety of old cars—fifteen-year-old Honda Civics, twenty-year-old Volvo and Subaru wagons, a few pick-ups, a Yugo, a '75 Gremlin, and a '68 GTO—several VW busses, assorted minivans, and a school bus with its emergency door removed, all covered with peace signs and bumper stickers that were difficult to read under a layer of white dust. He rolled down his window and heard chanting ahead. Large red letters were painted on the windows of the school bus—BE NICE. When he rounded the curve he saw the flicker of campfires. The campers must have seen his headlights, because the chanting ceased. Ten yards from the Great Door, as the Starlights called their main entrance, a line of a dozen young men, holding hands as if playing Red Rover, stretched across the road. Blevins halted the car inches from them and got out.

"Welcome, brother," they said in unison.

Blevins knew that this invitation was not sincere. He was a *leo*, law enforcement officer, and considered unfriendly by the Starlights.

"I'm Major Bombardi. Someone here reported a possible dead body."

"Not possible. Actual," said a young man in the center of the line. He wore the customary dreadlocks and a heavy shirt that looked like coarse wool. "I'm Tock. I remember you from last year. The beast chaser was found dead in his camp."

"Beast chaser?"

"The sasquatch hunter. This way."

The phalanx of young men broke rank to allow Blevins to follow Tock into the camp. Tock pointed to a cluster of people sitting on a fallen pine and staring at Blevins. "The one with the funny hat found him."

All the hats looked funny to Blevins. Some were the loose, tam-like woven caps worn by Rastafarians (although these were all white kids, mostly middle-class suburbanites), and others looked like they were pulled from the pages of Dr. Seuss. A Cat in the Hat boy arose from the group and approached. Blevins guessed him to be about nineteen years old. His lower lip was pierced with what appeared to be a dog whistle.

"What's your name, son?" Blevins asked.

The kid looked at Tock before he answered. "Ricky."

"You found the body?"

Ricky glanced at Tock again. "Yeah. He's out there by that trail."

"Wait here." Blevins went to his car. He retrieved the whiskey bottle from under the seat, placed it to his lips, and took a long pull. He radioed the department and told Maggie to send two of his detectives and returned to find Tock whispering to Ricky and wagging his finger in the boy's face. "OK," Blevins said. "Take me to him."

This was the warmest February on record throughout the country but especially in Florida. Temperatures had been near 90 the entire month with high humidity, feeling more like July than winter. Blevins guessed the temperature then at 10 PM to be in the upper 70s. The slight breeze offered little relief. After walking the trail a couple of hundred yards he rolled up his shirtsleeves.

The camp was in a clearing a few yards off the trail. Ricky pointed towards the rear of the tent. "He's back there."

A man lay on the ground face up about ten feet from the tent. Blevins looked him over with his flashlight: khaki shorts, hiking boots, a tee shirt with a picture of a chambered nautilus, dirt and leaves on his face and chest, eyes open. Blevins placed his hand on the man's neck: cold, no pulse.

"How did you find him?" Blevins asked.

"I just looked down," Ricky said.

"I mean, why were you out here, and is this how he was when you arrived?"

Rickey looked at Tock. Tock nodded. "A regular was chasing me," Ricky said. "I knew where the beast chaser was camping and wanted him to, well, I thought he might, protect me. He has a gun."

So far Blevins knew this much: The boy's ordinary name meant that he was a newcomer or temporary traveler. When a Starlight is officially accepted, he or she is newly dubbed by the elders. The young women get hippie-sounding names like "Earth Sister" and the young men nonsense syllables like "Blash" or "Nis." Also, a local person, a "regular," must have had a squabble with Ricky, and Ricky fled. Finally, Ricky and probably others had some sort of relationship, perhaps friendly, to this camper who, Tock said, was looking for a sasquatch.

"Tell me the whole story," Blevins said. "Do you know who this regular is?"

"I think his name is Mango," Tock said. "Big, giant guy. He started some trouble with us last year."

"Mingo," Blevins said. "Mingo Mauser. I remember last year's incident. What was the trouble this time?"

Tock said, "Ricky and the regular were fighting over a girl—"

"That's not true!" Ricky said. He looked at Tock and then at the ground. "Sorry. I mean, he, the regular, was bothering an outlier girl, and I asked him to leave her alone. He pushed me hard. I almost fell. He's a real big guy and I thought he was going to hit me." Ricky took a deep breath and adjusted his hat to sit farther down upon his forehead. "We don't believe in violence so I ran but he chased me. I thought he would give up soon cause he's kind of old and has a big gut, but he just kept coming after me. He was hollering, 'Stop you little bitch!' and 'I'll gut you like a she-bear!' I was near the beast chaser's camp so I ran there cause like I said I thought he might protect me."

Starlights back at their compound began to chant again.

"I was yelling 'help' when I got there, but I didn't see him nowhere," Ricky said. "Mother Moon was bright enough that I found the beast chaser's camp real easy even though there weren't no fires or lanterns burning. I was real afraid that he wasn't there and that the regular was going to kill me. Then I saw the dead guy lying there. I kept yelling but he didn't move so I kicked him but he didn't wake up." He put his hand on his crotch and bounced on his toes. "Can I take a pee?"

"Sure," Blevins said. "But step a few yards to the other side of the trail. This is a crime scene."

Ricky stepped a few yards away to a tree. Blevins could hear the piss splashing against the tree trunk.

"Did you see any of this?" Blevins asked Tock.

"No. Some others did. Harst and, I think, Lut was with him. And the outlier."

"I'll need to speak with them sooner or later. Know anything about this outlier?"

Tock spat on the ground. "No. Just saw her today."

Ricky returned, rubbing his hands on his chambray shirttail.

"OK, son, tell me what happened then."

Ricky shot a glance at Tock. "Then the regular was here," Ricky said. "He was panting hard but still could say 'I'm gonna fuck you bad, bitch.' But I said 'Look' and pointed at the dead guy. The regular squatted down beside him and rolled him over on his back. He laughed a little and said, 'Good thing for you.' I didn't know whether he was talking to me or the beast chaser. Then the regular stood up, took a few breaths, and I think he winked at me. Then he just walked back into the woods like nothing happened."

"Did you return to the camp immediately?"

"Yes. I came back and told Tock."

Blevins turned to Tock. "Did you call the department right away?"

"We tried," Tock said. "It's hard to get cell phone service out here. A bunch of us tried. Water Friend walked down the road until she got service and called 911."

A gust moved through the forest. Some of the Starlights whooped, perhaps believing the wind bore a woodland spirit. Blevins stood up. "Let's go back to your camp. I need to call in."

At the camp the Starlights clustered around fires. Someone threw a burning branch into the air that slammed to the ground spraying sparks. Girls squealed and scampered, boys laughed, and a couple of dogs—small, rounded ones favored by the privileged, not the curs that roam the gone-natural yards of Forest folk—yelped and sought cover. The festivities were not too different from bonfire parties Blevins remembered from high school, except instead of pastel-painted banners and chants of unity, those of Blevins' youth of forty years earlier sported Confederate flags and Lynyrd Skynyrd anthems.

Headlights shown from down the road. The car approached and stopped behind Blevins's. The lights remained on. The Evidence Division's detectives would not have had time to arrive, so Blevins assumed one of the patrolling deputies had heard the dispatch and came out to help. He walked out to the cars.

"Star light, star bright, what's them dip shits up to tonight?" Deputy Hendricks asked as he stepped to the front of Blevins's car.

"Hey, Maynard," Blevins said. "They found a dead camper out in the woods."

"One of them?"

"No. I just took a look. Lone male camper, probably in his forties."

"You need me to help out, Major? But you do all the talking, all right? These stink-ass sumbitches give me the fidgets."

"You're not alone," Blevins said. "Stay for a while. A couple of detectives should be here shortly. We probably can't do much tonight but tape the area. Somebody'll need to guard it until we can make a good sweep in the morning. You up for it?"

"Stay out here with these freaks?"

"The scene's outside their camp. They seem a little spooked by it, so I doubt any of them will even be near you. Maybe you'll enjoy the singing."

"Hell I will."

★ ★ ★ ★ ★ ★ ★ ★ ★ ★ ★ ★ ★ ★ ★ ★

Sheriff Todd's office was lined with plaques and certificates. Behind the desk hung the largest frame, holding a twenty-four by twenty inch photo of the Sheriff as a young deputy shaking hands with former Governor Lawton Chiles. Todd had received a commendation for bravery from a shootout in a failed pharmacy robbery. He had killed both perps and taken a bullet in the stomach. No civilians were harmed.

The Sheriff was on his third cup of coffee at 6:45 AM when Blevins rapped on his open door.

"Morning, Ash," Blevins said.

"It's been morning all night for me. This damn budget won't let me get a wink of sleep. Been up since three, here since four. Hear me? Have a seat, Blevins. What's all this with them Starlights this time?"

Blevins sat in a cordovan leather chair in front of the desk and told the Sheriff about the night before.

"Mingo Mauser again," Ashley said. "You think he had something to do with it, or them Starlights?"

"I haven't heard from Dewitt and Haynes yet. I'm on my way back out there now."

"What you going out there for? They're good detectives. Let them do their job. These goddamn politicians in Tallahassee say they're all for law enforcement and then they tell me I got to make a fifteen percent cut. You know how big this county is. How am I supposed to cover this place when I had to cut people last year? Then they said on the news this morning that a tropical storm suddenly popped up and is probably heading this way. A tropical storm in February. Can you believe that horse shit? I got enough things to worry about without you not staying here minding the Major Crimes department."

"Ash, I've researched the Starlights and know more about them than anybody here. And we haven't had a homicide in the Forest in years. Plenty of other shit, but I think the Forest residents are going to be reluctant to say much if they know anything. Especially if Mingo is in fact involved. Hell, most of them'd rather be arrested than to testify against him. You know I know these people. My region for twelve years. Crews can help out with the desk."

Ashley threw two Rolaids tablets into his mouth. He stared at Blevins for a few breaths. "How's your, um, condition?"

Blevins clinched his jaw. "I have an appointment tomorrow. My shrink thinks I might be ready to come off my meds. Besides, he said last time that maybe I need a change of pace, like maybe being more hands-on with investigations."

Ashley crunched the tablets with his mouth open. "Well." He swallowed, then took a gulp of coffee. He stared at Blevins for several heartbeats. "This might damn well come back to bite me in the balls, but I'm gonna let you do this. Now, we got to face the hairy-ass elephant in the room. I know you think I hold a grudge against you. Hell, everybody thinks that. Truth be told, I probably do. I don't want nobody, not *no* damn body thinking that I'm giving you some shit hole assignment to get at you. Hear me? Morale is bad enough with all my men worried about whether they'll have a job next fiscal year."

"Look, Ashley—"

"The minute I hear any grumbling, from *any* damn body, I'm pulling you off. You make damn sure everybody knows you begged me to do this. Got it?"

The chair arms squeaked under Blevins's grip. "I got it." He stood.

"One more thing." The Sheriff ate another tablet. "Take that new kid Moreno with you. She's a bright girl, top out at CF, and I want to see her groomed for something. Something else I'm catching heat about with not enough blacks being promoted. Can't hurt it's a woman, too. Hear me? I talked to her a few times, and I think she might make it."

"Yes sir," Blevins said and turned toward the door.

"Blevins," Ashley said. "You know I really care here—anything on your daughter?"

Blevins halted but did not turn to face the Sheriff. "No," he said and walked out.

★ ★ ★ ★ ★ ★ ★ ★ ★ ★ ★ ★ ★ ★ ★

Water oaks and longleaf pines flanked the narrow dirt road. The matted undergrowth of ferns and palmettos was overdue for a controlled burn. Two mobile homes, one without its tires, were anchored along the half-mile stretch of road. Blevins pulled into the yard at the end of the road in front of a green A-frame house. On the side by a clutch of brown azalea bushes a late model Dodge pickup was hooked to a trailer carrying an airboat. Blevins finished his coffee, and he and Roberta Moreno walked to the porch. Blevins knocked on the door. He waited a moment and knocked again. "Mingo!" he called.

"Yo!" came a voice from behind the house at the same time that a dog barked. Blevins and Moreno walked to the back to see Mingo emerge from a tin-roofed shed. He was shirtless and held a large knife. He was still a hulking figure, but he looked as if he had lost a few inches off his gut since Blevins had last run into him several months earlier. A black and white dog that appeared to be a mix of a Boston terrier and a fox squirrel hopped and barked beside him.

"Well kiss my sanctified ass if it ain't the good Major Blevins. Come take a look, Shaky. And do something about this son-of-a-bitching sooner of yours."

A man about 30 years old emerged to stand beside Mingo. The man also had a knife and wore a white tee shirt with the arms cut off and a large red stain on the front.

Mingo stepped towards Blevins. "What you want with me, Major?"

Blevins stared at the blood covering Mingo's arms up to his elbows. "I understand you found a body last night."

"You had to bring a helper to ask me that?"

"This is Deputy Moreno. I thought she should become acquainted with some of the county's more respected citizens. The Starlights said you were having a fuss with them last night and followed a kid to a tent where a body was found."

Mingo wiped the bloody knife on his camouflage pants leg. "You listen to them heathens? Yeah, I was out there witnessing to them. I got the Lord now, you know. That's the only thing keeping me civil towards you right now. You know—love your enemies."

"I'm glad to hear it. Did you know the dead man?"

"Talked to him a time or two. Crazy. Looking for the skunk ape. We had a friendly conversation when I was out . . . bird watching."

The man behind Mingo threw back his head and snorted. His

blue and green striped welder's cap slipped to the back of his head. "Hahnk! We seen us a bunch of birds, didn't we, Mingo? Heeyoh!" Blevins saw a blue birthmark on the man's forehead that resembled India.

"Shut the fuck up, Shaky," Mingo said. "And I done told you about that damn shit eater."

Shaky lifted the yapping dog, took it into the shed, and returned without it.

"What did you and the skunk ape guy talk about?" Blevins asked.

Mingo slipped a pouch of Red Man chewing tobacco from his back pocket. His took his time shaping a wad with his bloody fingers and placing it into his cheek. He held the pouch toward the deputy.

"No thank you," Moreno said. She looked to Blevins as if wondering about proper protocol.

"You don't know what you're missing, princess" Mingo said as he returned the pouch to his pocket. "So I was telling the guy about how skunk apes is demons of the devil and he should get the hell out of them woods. He didn't take too well to my advice." He spat tobacco onto the ground just beside Blevins's shoe. "We about done here, Blevins? I got to finish cleaning them squirrels."

The other man snorted again. "Squirrels."

"Shaky, get back in the shed," Mingo said. Shaky obeyed.

"Pretty big knife for cleaning squirrels," Blevins said.

"I only shoot the big ones."

"What went on between you and the Starlights last night?"

Mingo threw his knife down. It stuck straight up in the dirt. "Am I under investigation? I done told you I was witnessing. Everyone of them ass fuckers is hell bound, and I got a duty to Lord Jesus Christ my savior to make sure they hear the Word at least once. Now, one of them started in on me and words was said. Next thing I know he takes off and me after him. We found the dead guy and I come on home. That's the whole of it."

"They told me you got into a spat over a girl."

"Bull shit!" Mingo shouted and reached down for his knife.

Moreno went into a crouch and drew her pistol on Mingo.

"Holster that weapon, Deputy!" Blevins said.

The deputy stood erect and returned the pistol to its holster. She took three deep breaths, exhaling slowly through rounded lips as if blowing out a candle. Her hand remained on the 9mm's grip.

Mingo pushed the knife to the hilt into the ground, slid it up and down in the dirt, wiped the blade on his pants again, and placed the knife into the leather sheath at his belt. "Got a live one there, Blevins. Anybody, even a woman, who pulls a gun on me usually don't get away so easy. I strike like lightening."

A thud emitted from the shed. "Goddamnit!" Shaky yelled. "Ooowee hell! Fucking shitass rope! "

Blevins moved toward the shed.

"Stay out of there!" Mingo said. He sidled three strides to try to block the view. "This is private property!"

Blevins made a side-step to get a glimpse around Mingo and into the shed. Shaky was standing over a mound of black fur. Shaky looked back. He squatted with his arms extended, trying to hide something.

"You have a bear in there, Mingo," Blevins said.

"I didn't kill it," Mingo said. "and you need a warrant anyhow."

"No, I don't," Blevins said. "It's in plain view."

Blevins approached the open shed. The broken rope attached to the bear's back legs had become detached from where the animal had hung from a wooden rafter holding the tin roof. A bucket had overturned, spilling blood and viscera. A few feet away another bear was chained upside down to an engine hoist. Its stomach was cut open, and most of the hide was skinned down and hanging over the bear's face like a robe. The dog, tied to a chain, gnawed on a kidney.

Deputy Moreno began to cough. She spread a handkerchief over her mouth and gagged. She bent over with her hands on her knees and vomited.

"You know the penalty for killing bears, Mingo?" Blevins said.

"Damn right I do. Like I done said, I ain't the one who killed them bear. I found all two of them dead in the woods on my way home last night. They had arrows in them. I don't shoot no bow and arrow."

"It's illegal to have them."

"What the hell sense does that law make? They just gonna rot in the woods. You think it's easy making a living as a fishing guide? I don't have a government job like you that actually hands you a steady check, whether you earn it or not."

Blevins turned to Moreno. "You OK, Deputy?"

Roberta rocked back onto her heels and wiped her mouth. "Yes sir. Must've been those greasy eggs I had for breakfast."

"Let's go," Blevins said. "I'll be back, Mingo. In the meantime, you try to think of anyone you know who might've wanted that guy dead. Now, I have to notify the Game Commission about these bears." Blevins and Moreno began to walk away.

"Fuck all y'all," Mingo said. "You got a murderer on the loose, and you got nothing better to do than pester me about a few pounds of meat?" He followed Blevins. "Say, how's that monk brother of yours?"

Blevins continued to walk, "Left the monastery years ago. He might be a Buddhist, so I reckon he's hell bound, too."

Mingo laughed. "Then you tell him I said 'namaste, motherfucker.' And don't forget, at least *you* got a brother."

★ ★ ★ ★ ★ ★ ★ ★ ★ ★ ★ ★ ★ ★

Blevins looked at the thick undergrowth of ferns among the pines just beyond the sandy shoulder as the department vehicle sped along State Road 40. This part of the Forest could use a controlled burn, he thought, but he was sure the Parks people would consider it too risky in this drought.

"Major," Moreno said. "About back there. Can I just say—"

"Forget it," Blevins said. "Nothing to be embarrassed about. Happens to everybody."

"I just want you to know that I had no problem pulling my firearm and preparing to discharge it. My training kicked in, and I was in fact relieved, no, proud, that my reflexes, my muscle memory, followed procedure."

"As you should be. You sensed a highly volatile situation, and you reacted appropriately. Good job. Only because of my experience with Mauser did I know there was no danger. You couldn't have known that."

Moreno held her hat in her lap. She spun it around like a steering wheel. "It's just that, you know, any time I've ever pointed my firearm it's been in training scenarios. This was the first time in the field, and the adrenaline got pumping and my nerves were on high alert and my stomach just couldn't, well, you know."

"Of course. Listen to me, you did fine."

"It won't happen again, Sir."

"Yes it will. Many times. When it gets where it doesn't bother you at all, that's when you worry."

"Thank you, Sir," Moreno said. "Now, one other thing. Did I detect some bad blood back there?"

"You mean between Mingo and me," Blevins said, "not what spilled out that bucket, right? Yeah, I've known him about all my life. Played football together at Forest High, then at the University of Florida. Things soured over the years."

"Let me guess. He was a lineman."

"Offense and defense. He was two-forty-five and solid muscle. Almost as fast as our running backs. Led the state two years in sacks. I was a receiver. I got a small football scholarship to UF and took out a mound of loans. He got a full ride and probably would have made All-American but partied too much and flunked out our freshman year."

"But you finished your degree, right?"

"Yeah. Then got a research assistantship and went to grad school to study philosophy."

"Grad school? So, does that mean you're like, *Doctor* Bombardi?"

Blevins took a pack of chewing gum from his shirt pocket, gave Moreno a stick, then folded one into his own mouth. "Not quite. I decided the academic life wasn't quite for me after all. But that was a long time ago."

"One other thing, Major, if you don't mind me asking. What was that remark Mingo made about your brother?"

Blevins turned on the car's air conditioner. "That's a little complicated. He lost his own brother in a bar fight a long time ago. Blames me, probably anybody else, for having one, I guess." He pointed to the dashboard. "Look at this. Only 9:30

in the morning and it's 79 degrees. Well, the detectives have been at the scene for a while now. Let's see if they turned up anything. I also want to talk to the Starlights some more."

"Now, can you fill me in on these Starlights?"

"I take it you're not from here, Moreno."

"Originally, Sir, but my mother died. Actually, she was killed, when I was five. She was black, and my father was Cuban. I've always thought that had something to do with him just letting my mother's family take me. So, I lived with my aunt in Atlanta. Then my grandparents—my mother's parents—weren't doing so well and my aunt moved back down to take care of them, and I came back with her. I'd just graduated from high school, and I enrolled at the college and got interested in criminal justice. I got my associate's and went straight into the police academy. Just finished up last semester."

"You lived here in town when you were small?"

"Yes, Sir. Right off Martin Luther King Avenue, near where N. H. Jones Elementary is."

"Old Martí City."

"Sir?"

"Named for the Cuban poet and revolutionary Jose Martí. Ocala had a cigar industry for a while, and Martí came here just as he'd done in Miami and Tampa trying to get the Cuban workers to support the revolution against Spain. Was your father from those Cuban families?"

A deputy came on the radio informing the communication center that he'd stopped a probable drunk who was weaving from lane to lane on US 441.

"I'm not sure, Sir. I think I remember my father talking about my grandfather—wait, maybe great-grandfather—living here many years ago. If my grandfather or great-grandfather, whatever, lived here before, he must've moved back, because I know that my father was born in Cuba and came here as a boy. What I remember most about my father was him talking about Cuba all the time, how it was a paradise with the sweetest fruits, brightest flowers, prettiest birds, and the most beautiful women in the world. I dreamed I'd someday go there and live in a hut on the beach and be happy ever after. My aunt wouldn't let me talk about Cuba. One time I brought home a library book about it, and she whipped my behind with a fly swatter."

Blevins adjusted an air conditioner vent to blow directly onto his face. "Funny, isn't it? Everybody thinks of Florida as a Shangri-La except for the Cubans, who pine to return to their promised land. You should go there, Moreno. The travel embargo was lifted—what?—two years ago?"

"I'd need to save up some if I did that. What about you? You've probably lived your whole life here, huh?"

"Yes. My great-great-grandfather, my mother's great-grandfather—she gave me his first name—moved here from South Carolina. Much of north Florida was settled by South Carolinians. Both Marion and Sumter Counties are named for Revolutionary War generals from there. My old man, though, was from Louisville, Kentucky. He grew up on a horse farm up there then moved here to start his own." Blevins pointed off the road to the edge of the trees. "That a bear?" He pressed the brake. "Nope. Just a dead dog, a black and tan." He resumed speed.

"And your name, 'Bombardi.' Italian, right?"

"Probably, although my old man claimed that his grandfather came to the States from Ulster and spoke only Scots, and when he told the emigration people his name, they couldn't understand him and wrote down what it sounded like to them. I looked around a little bit but couldn't find a Scottish or Irish name that sounded anything like 'Bombardi.' I think my old man or maybe his old man just made it up because of prejudice against the Italians. Anyway, you asked about the Starlights."

"Yes, Sir."

"The Starlight Family of Cosmic Energy is a moveable feast of waifs, starry-eyed new agers, bunch of spoiled rich kids who decided to swallow some quasi-pantheistic religion and a bunch of hallucinogens. Started in 1998 by a handful of Y2K nuts, they have a circuit of national parks where they stay depending upon the time of year. In spring it's in the Great Smokies, late summer Yellowstone, winter here. Some others in between. Most of them are official members who end up staying with the group an average of four years before they finally get homesick or run through their trust funds. They have a formalized pecking order, partly based on how long they've been members, partly on elections, some on how far the wind blows a leaf with their name written on it. Three quarters are in their 20s, most of the rest are in their 30s, a few in their 40s. There's always some temporaries, 'outliers' they call them, usually runaways. Most outliers aren't interested in membership, and after a couple of months drop out and end up on the streets of some city, usually drugged out or hooking. But while they're in the parks they're not much trouble. Get a little loud at night, which aggravates other campers, but they're always careful with their fires, and they leave the campsite immaculate when they move on. The real problem is in town. They thumb rides in and shoplift most of their food. You'll also see them sitting by the road with cardboard signs asking for food or panhandling in parking lots."

"Any violence, burglaries?"

The deputy on the radio reported that he was arresting the driver, a member of the school board, for driving while intoxicated.

"No. Sometimes a domestic squabble over accusations of stolen weed. One dumbass a couple of years ago even called the department about his weed being stolen. No burglaries, but like I was saying, they're experts at slipping a few items from a gas station. Two or three'll distract the clerk and another'll stuff his pockets."

"You sure know a lot of things."

"Well, I've been around a while."

Moreno chuckled. "Not what I meant. You have a lot to say."

"Oh. You mean pedantic."

"Yeah. I wasn't going to say it like that, but, anyway, how'd you come to know so much about the Starlights?"

Blevins took the curve on the macadam road a little faster than he normally would have. "They're right up ahead. We'll check with our guys first, then do some questioning."

★ ★ ★ ★ ★ ★ ★ ★ ★ ★ ★ ★ ★ ★ ★

Yellow "Do Not Cross" tape stretched between trees to cordon off a rough circle of about thirty yards in diameter. The two plain-clothed detectives and a park ranger stood near the tent while three young deputies of the Evidence Division placed items into boxes and plastic bags. No Starlights were nearby.

Blevins and Moreno joined the detectives. They exchanged "good mornings," and Blevins introduced the new deputy to Detectives Dewitt and Haynes and Park Ranger Fleming. They shook hands as the other deputies, two young men and a young woman, went about their business collecting items.

"Not much to go on here," Dewitt said. "Nothing in the tent seems to be tampered with. A bunch of high tech equipment—cameras, infrared binoculars, solar powered laptop. He had some journals we can go through."

"ID?" Blevins asked.

"Yeah. Fleming can tell you more about him," the detective said.

The park ranger lit a cigarette. "Dr. Peter Boykin, from UWF. Cryptozoologist. Bigfoot hunter. Got here two weeks ago, told me what he was up to. Said there hasn't been a 'thoroughly scientific' attempt to track the skunk ape, so he hoped to be the one to find it. Got a dozen or so motion-activated cameras and sound recorders set up out there. He talked to some locals about their so-called sightings. Poor crazy bastard."

"Did he have any run-ins with anybody you know of?" Blevins asked.

"Didn't mention any. Said he'd got some good evidence. Showed me a picture that he said was promising. He got a little huffy when I said it looked like a bear to me."

Blevins turned to the detectives. "What about the body? Trauma?"

"Take a look at this," Haynes said.

The body was turned back onto its stomach. "Looks like he was dead on his stomach, then somebody turned him over," Haynes said.

Blevins nodded. "He was on his back last night. The Starlight who found him said a local, Mingo Mauser, was here and turned him on his back."

"This seems to be what killed him," Dewitt said. He pointed to a wound on the back of the corpse's head. "Something small and blunt hit him hard but unlikely a bullet. And no exit wound."

"Like he got knocked with a ball peen hammer," Haynes said. "We found a ball bearing, probably stainless steel, a couple of feet away," Dewitt said. "Maybe half a pound."

Blevins squatted to inspect the wound. It was round and about an inch in diameter just above where the skull connects to the spine. Blood had trickled out and dried on the back of his neck.

"You'd have to hurl a ball bearing like, what's that pitcher, I think he's with the Reds, they call him the Cuban Missile?" Haynes asked.

"Aroldis Chapman," Dewitt said.

"That's him. You have to throw like Chapman to kill a man with that ball bearing."

"I saw this documentary about fastball pitchers, and it said that they didn't measure them in the same ways. If they used the same machines or whatever, Nolan Ryan would've been the fastest, at about 120 miles a hour or something like that."

"So, you think Nolan Ryan killed this sorry fucker?"

"Kiss my ass," Dewitt said. "Like I said earlier, what about a sling shot?"

Fleming dropped his cigarette but to the ground, pressed it out with his boot. "Those wrist rockets are pretty powerful. You know, the ones with the rubber tubing? But they usually shoot little pellets, not something that big, right?"

"I guess we'll have to wait on the coroner's report," Blevins said. "Get all this stuff to the department. Go through his emails. Look through the journals. See if he had a voice recorder. This has the potential of a media frenzy—'Who wanted the skunk ape man killed? What did he know that someone wanted to keep covered up?' So let's try to work fast and solve this before anything like that starts. I'll talk to the Starlights again."

"Better hurry on that," Ranger Fleming said. "The weather report said that tropical storm's picking up strength and heading straight for us. We might have to evacuate everyone from the park."

"How many Starlights are here?" Blevins asked.

"Biggest group we ever had," Fleming said. "I reckon about a thousand."

Blevins stood up. "Worse comes to worst, we'll find somewhere to shelter them. Bus them to that old convention center on route 19. By the way, you see anyone out here with a bow?"

Fleming fanned his face with his big ranger's hat. "I wish like hell I had. We found two dead bears the other day, arrows in them. Found some ground round near them, like somebody was baiting them."

"Add two more bear casualties," Blevins said. "That Mingo Mauser I mentioned?"

"I know him, all right," Fleming said.

"I found him cleaning two bears in his shed this morning. Said he found them dead. Arrows in them, too. I already called the Game Commission. They'll slap a pretty heavy fine on him."

"Oh yeah," Fleming said. "They'll hit him hard. And you know what else? The Silver River rangers just found half a dozen dead monkeys. Arrows. They've probably notified your office about it."

"I heard about that," Moreno said. "Wonder why anybody'd do that?"

Fleming laughed. "Crazy bastards everywhere. I just wish they'd space themselves out instead of convening here all at once."

★ ★ ★ ★ ★ ★ ★ ★ ★ ★ ★ ★ ★ ★

At the Starlight camp, Blevins found Tock and had him locate the others who witnessed the altercation between Mingo and Ricky.

"The regular was talking with the outlier girl about some religious stuff," Harst said. "They weren't arguing. She seemed to be agreeing with his end of times talk, but they were getting all excited like they were looking forward to the end of the world."

"I thought they were getting mad at first," Lut said. "I can see why Ricky told the regular to settle down."

"Can you be a little more specific about they were saying?" Blevins asked.

Harst retied his bandana around his dread locks. "I couldn't follow it. Lots of Jesus talk. Something about signs and the beast."

"Revelation," Lut said. "My mother used to make me read the Bible. They were talking about signs of the apocalypse. The outlier was all up on some preacher, a TV preacher I think, and the regular must have known the guy too. She said the wrath of God was here."

"Oh yeah," Harst said. "I remember her saying 'I strike like lightening.'"

Blevins glanced at Moreno. Moreno nodded.

"Now this Ricky tried to intervene, right?" Blevins asked.

Someone played a ukulele nearby. Singing began. *We are all from the one and the one gives to all.*

Harst and Lut got out of their hemp hammocks. "We need to go, Sheriff," Harst said. "Like I said, Ricky asked the regular to calm down, the regular shoved him—"

"Right into me," Lut said. "Splashed my tea all over me."

"—Ricky ran. That's all we know. Now we need to go."

"No one tried to help Ricky?" Blevins asked.

"Look, Sheriff," Harst said. "The Family is peaceful. Beside, Ricky's not a member."

"One more thing," Blevins said. He took out his cell phone and found the photo files. "Either of you recognize this girl?"

"No," both Lut and Harst said immediately. They left to join the singers, now a group of a hundred or more. As others passed by to join in, Blevins stopped them and showed the photo. All shook their heads and continued by, giving no more than a cursory glance.

"Let's get out of here," Blevins said to Moreno, "before we get trapped in the throng."

★★★★★ ★★★★★ ★★★★★

Blevins stopped the department car in the sandy parking lot of one of the few restaurants in the Forest. Moreno pointed at the sign.

"Krazy Karla's Kitchen," she said. "Are you kidding me? KKK?"

Blevins laughed. "I'm sure it never occurred to Karla. To be honest, I guess I never noticed."

"What?" Moreno asked. "How white you got to be not to notice?" Moreno lifted her hat from her lap and placed it on her head. "I'm sorry, Sir. I meant no disrespect."

"I know."

"I'll bet, though," Moreno said, "that after I leave, she'll change it to 'Krazy Karla's Kracker—with a k—Kitchen.'"

The little seating room was nearly full. Twelve customers for lunch had Karla hopping, refilling coffee for a table of four septuagenarians and sorting the orders for a crew of linemen from Florida Power. When Blevins opened the screen door and the hinges creaked, he heard Karla growl "shit."

"Oh, Blevins," Karla said. "I'm sorry. I'm just wore out and it's only midday. Seat yourselves."

Karla disappeared into the back while Blevins and Moreno took the table by the window beside the old locals.

"Major Bombardi," said one of the old men. "Well kiss my narrow ass. I ain't been seeing you in a coon's—" he paused, looking at Moreno—"blue moon." He wore a yellow, straw fedora with the brim turned up.

"Why you out from behind that desk?" another asked, stroking the long, gray beard that rested on his chest. "They ain't knocked you down to buck private, is they?"

"That might be a blessing," Blevins said.

"I hear y'all found a cold one out in them woods," said a third. He chewed an unlit cigar.

Blevins scanned the menu, a single sheet of paper with a drawing in the margin of a smiling catfish holding a fishing cane. "News travels fast out here," Blevins said.

"That's about all been moving fast out here," said the fedora man. "That and Karla's coffee been running through me." The old men chuckled and snorted.

"They say he was a scientist," the bearded man said.

"Scientist your crusty ass!" said the fourth old man. He wore a mesh cap with "Nasty Ornery and Mean!" written across the front. "Lunatic, I say. Looking for the skunk ape. Might as well ought to been looking for my million dollars."

"Don't start your shit," said the cigar chewer. "You know damn well I seen that stink ass monster."

"Of course you did, Preston," said Nasty. "Just like the time you said you were in a bear fight when it turned out those scratches was from running through the briars from Tiny Goodman when he caught you with his wife."

"OK, I might've lied about that one," Cigar said. "But the skunk ape? I know what I saw."

"Where did you see him, sir?" Moreno asked.

"Don't be egging him on, sweetheart," Fedora said. "He's the lyingest cuss who ever shat behind two heels."

"How you mean, 'shat'?" Nasty asked.

"That's past tense for 'shit,' you stupid ass," Fedora said. "But you don't be knowing what a past tense is, do you?"

Nasty pushed his cap to the back of his head. "You think I never slept in tents? But I ain't never passed no shit, excuse me, shat, in them."

Karla returned. "How you been, Blevins?"

"Fine, Karla. The real question is, when you going to retire?"

"I can't never retire. At least Lance cooks for me now. I thought it'd be better outen the kitchen, but I be dog if I don't nearly about walk my legs off. I see you got some help today."

"This is Deputy Moreno, new to the department."

Moreno nodded to Karla. "I reckon she is," she said. "Looks like she's barely old enough to chew her own food. Ha! Now, what you officers want for your dinner?"

"I'll take a catfish basket and some tea," Blevins said.

"You got a salad, just veggies?" Moreno asked.

"You know it, darling," Karla said. "I can make you a special one. You can't believe it, but you know what's real good on a salad? Bread-and-butter pickles and roasted rutabagas. Then I put my special apple cider vinegar and blood orange dressing on it, and honey, you ain't never had nothing like it."

"That sure sounds, I guess, interesting," Moreno said.

"Don't nobody hardly ever ask for a salad here no more," Karla said. "I'll take a special pleasure in making it for you." She put her hand on Moreno's shoulder. "And don't you listen to them old fools over there, honey. They ain't good for nothing but telling lies and emptying coffee cups."

"I don't lie, Karla," Beard said. "Except if I said you ain't the prettiest thing *in* this world." The other old men threw back their heads and laughed. Fedora's hat fell to the floor. He grunted as he tried to retrieve it. Moreno picked it up and handed it to him.

"Thank you, sweety," Fedora said. "Say, Blevins, you ought to be talking to old Fox Renfroe at the fire tower. Anything funny going on out in them woods, he generally knowing about it."

"Already planned on it," Blevins said.

The power company linemen arose from their table, and as they walked to the door, one stopped at Blevin's table. "Excuse me, sir. We weren't sure who we should tell about it, but we were out on a call this morning—a sweetgum fell on some lines—when we found a dead bear. It had an arrow in it. That's how I spotted it, a bright orange arrow sticking up. Me and Jimbo over there went to take a closer look, and when we did, we thought we saw somebody run off into the woods. Small, might've been a girl."

"Where was this?" Blevins asked.

"Second dirt road on the right out from here. I believe it's called Scrub Gulley Road. About a mile down it you'll see the fallen tree there. The bear's about thirty yards off the road."

"Thank you, son," Blevins said. "I'll notify the rangers and the game commission. See any raw meat or other food, something that might've been used for bait, anywhere around?"

"Well, actually, yes. Some chicken parts on the ground."

"Any details about this person you saw? Clothes? Hair color?"

"No sir. It might not even've been a girl. Just looked kind of like it to me and Jimbo."

"Here—write your name and phone number on this pad in case they want to talk to you."

"Yes sir," the lineman said. "We're not going to get in any trouble are we? I mean, we did plan to call somebody soon."

"Nothing to worry about, son," Blevins said. "Here's my card. Call me if you remember anything else. Y'all have a good day."

Karla brought out the plates of food and set them before Blevins and Moreno.

Moreno looked at her salad. She shifted a piece of lettuce with her fork and saw an orange rutabaga cube. "Wow. That looks, actually, wonderful, Miss Karla."

"You enjoy it, sweetie," Karla said. "You did want tea, didn't you? Unsweetened, I'm thinking?"

"Yes, Ma'am. Thank you."

Karla lay two packets of artificial sweetener on the table and returned to the kitchen.

"There's more catfish here than I can eat," Blevins said.

"You're welcome to a piece."

Roberta sighed. "You have no idea how much I used to love catfish, but I haven't had any fried food since I started the academy."

"Just one little piece?"

Moreno chewed a piece of palm heart. "I might die in uniform, but it won't be from clogged arteries."

★ ★ ★ ★ ★ ★ ★ ★ ★ ★ ★ ★ ★ ★

Seven flights of steps zig-zagged to the cab atop the fire tower. Ranger Fox Renfroe leaned over the rail surrounding the cab and called for Blevins and Moreno to come up. Blevins rolled up his shirtsleeves and wiped his glasses on a handkerchief. "I wish we could get there standing here," he said, "but that's not likely to happen. Might as well head up."

On the fourth flight Blevins stopped to rest. His face was flushed. He panted.

"You OK, Major?" Moreno asked.

"Just this heat. Need to catch my breath." He wiped his sweaty face and neck with the bandana. "Let's go."

Renfroe met them at the top. "Lord, Blevins, don't you go catching a stroke on me. Get in here and sit down. The fan'll cool you off."

The cab felt ten degrees cooler than outside, probably down to about 80. "Can't believe this heat," Renfroe said. "And been dry as my pecker for a month." He looked at Moreno. "Oh, pardon me, young lady."

"This is Deputy Moreno," Blevins said. "Deputy, Ranger Renfroe."

"Pleased to meet you," Renfroe said. "Don't believe I've ever seen a female deputy out here in the woods. Now, like I was saying, prime conditions for fires. Lucky so far, though. What brings y'all out here, that dead scientist?"

Blevins unbuttoned his shirt to his navel. He wondered how Renfroe, in his late 60s and his belt buckled below his massive gut, managed the climb every day. "Yeah. Did you meet this guy?"

"He come up here asking about the skunk ape. I told him where people claimed to see it. Wanted to set up some cameras. I drove him around in the four-wheeler and helped him"

"I'd like to send a deputy or two out to gather those cameras. You mind taking them out to where you told the scientist to go?" Blevins asked.

"Don't mind at all. He seemed like a nice enough fellow, except he braced when I told him there weren't no substance to that old legend. Just backwoods people's imaginations. They can't be satisfied with the wonders the good Lord give us. Bears, bobcats. I'm of a mind there might even still be a panther out here. Sometimes I wonder if the skunk ape and bigfoot and all them things are hoaxes manufactured by the government to keep people distracted from something else, like, hell, I don't know, maybe UFOs or some kind of secret military operations. Any damn how, I told that fellow he ought to be looking for a panther if he wanted to do something worthwhile. Showed me some little sandwich bags with bits of hair and scat and asked me what I thought. I said probably coyotes. Those demon dogs are ruining this forest. I caught one worrying a gopher tortoise last week. I shot in the air to scare it off. I probably ought to've killed it."

"The game commission has been talking about doing just that," Blevins said. "They're wrecking the ecosystem."

"Lots of wrecking going on," Renfroe said. "And some of them Starlights were out here looking in the gopher holes. You know I got seven holes in this one clearing? Probably the most in one area anywhere. They's some what eats them old tortoises. The Seminoles used to throw them right on the fire. When the belly shell cracked, he was done, and they just scoop it out with a spoon like a stew. Hell, maybe they might not've had spoons back then. They was primitive as pure hell. Indians don't give a shit about nothing. At them reservations—I ain't never set foot in one, now—the government gives them everything, but them Indians don't put it to no use. Won't even turn on their spigots for free water. Shit right in their own yard." Renfroe took from his breast pocket a pipe that looked as if it had been rough hewed from a lightered knot, filled it with tobacco from small bag, and lit. "You know old Bim Mullins? He'd eat a gopher. Said he lost a little fyce rabbit dog and went out looking for him. Heard the dog growling but couldn't place him. Finally coursed the growling to a gopher hole. Bim reached in the hole and pulled the fyce out by a hind leg, and that dog was latched on a gopher! Bim started taking the dog out hunting for them old things. He'd shoot them in the head with this Yugoslavian rifle his son brought home from Bosnia. Used rounds with them Berdan primers that he swore by but I don't trust worth a shit. Cooked them gophers up with carrots and turnips. Said it was the best eatingest thing he ever put in his mouth. Now I've been poor all my life, but I never been so hard up that I'd eat them ugly ass things."

Blevins stood and leaned his face to the fan. The smoke from Renfroe's pipe smelled more like pine than tobacco. "Did you talk to the Starlights?"

"Hell no. I hollered at them and they took off to the road. I reckon they were thumbing their way to town to steal from the Walmart. Y'all ought to crack down on them. Ain't nothing but hoodlums. If any of my young'ns had run off like that, I'd've beat them half dead."

"Most of them are just messed up kids, Fox. You got any idea about who's killing the bears?"

Renfroe relit his pipe. "I must've sweat in my tobacco. Not burning good. Well, my first thought was them Starlights, but they've never done any real mischief out here. I doubt the ones looking for that gopher meant to harm it. But who the hell knows? What I can't figure out is how whoever's doing it killed two. There's people lived out here all their lives and never seen a bear but once or twice. They're real skiddish, you know. The bears *and* the people!" Renfroe laughed and punched Moreno in the shoulder. She winced and took a step away from the old man.

"Make that five, at least," Blevins said. "I found two at a local's home. He said he didn't do it. Some Florida Power linemen just told me they found another this morning. This hunter's pretty good at it."

"I'll be damn," Renfroe said. "Pretty coincidental, ain't it? The Starlights getting here and bears meeting up with arrows."

"I'll give you that. But they're sort of nature worshippers. Doesn't make sense."

Renfroe tapped his pipe into on the rail. "I ain't believing somebody been in the Sheriff's Department as long as you still looking for things to make sense."

* * * * * * * * * * * * * * * *

"I need to ask you a few things, Major," Moreno said.

Blevins drove towards town on Highway 40 at 85 miles per hour, twenty miles over the speed limit. "Shoot," he said.

"What, or maybe, who were you showing the Starlights on your phone?"

"Picture of a runaway. Might have joined up with them."

"Local?"

"Yes."

"Someone you knew?"

Blevins picked up the radio and told the dispatcher he was on the way in. "Tell my people I'm going to want to hear everything they've found out." He turned up the air conditioner. "That's an unrelated case."

"Yes, Sir," Moreno said, "but when Renfroe said something about what he'd do if his kids had run off, you kind of frowned. Just seemed to touch a nerve."

"No time for playing psychologist. Let's focus on this homicide."

"Yes, Sir. And I couldn't tell whether the ranger was talking about turtles or gophers."

"Gopher tortoise. Large tortoise that burrows into the ground, hence 'gopher.' They're protected. You really don't know very much about your birthplace, do you?"

"I guess not. And I've never heard of a skunk ape. You don't really think there's some kind of monster out here, do you?"

"I try to be open minded, but I'm skeptical about all the cryptozoology you see on TV and read in the papers. Hairy, apelike humanoids have been in the myths of probably every human culture for thousands of years. They represent our worst fear, that we're not separate from the animal kingdom."

Moreno chuckled. "My grandmother gets really upset when anyone mentions Bigfoot. She says it's just those 'evolution scientists' trying to prove a missing link and show that the Bible's not true."

"She's pretty religious, huh?"

"You can't believe. She watches televangelists, the worst ones, all the time. The only news she gets is from the Christian Broadcasting Network. Makes her paranoid. Thinks everybody's out to destroy Christianity."

"She'd have that in common with many of the folks out here."

"That'd be about all." Moreno leaned slightly to check the speedometer. Ninety. "No offense, Major, but the Forest looks like nothing but cracker-ville to me."

Blevins noticed Moreno leaning and slowed down to eighty. "You're right about that, Deputy. You know, don't you, that many white Floridians don't think of 'cracker' as a derogatory term?"

"I think my grandmother said something about that."

"They've invented a mythos about the term originating from the crack of cowmen's whips back before the fence laws. White people in Florida, especially poor ones or at least those whose ancestors were poor, whose families settled here, say, four or five generations ago, think of themselves as true Floridians and proudly call themselves crackers."

Moreno shook her head. "You really don't notice how much you, um, lecture, do you, Sir? Anyway, so, if I called you a cracker, you'd be okay with it?"

Blevins laughed. "Been on the job as long as I have, you're called everything imaginable. It'll happen to you, too. I've always been of the opinion that black people don't have any racial slurs for white people that have anywhere near the freight of the N word. So, in a way, it's a shame that they're robbed of 'cracker,' at least in Florida. Anyway, maybe we should assign you out here permanently as a kind of race relations liaison."

"I, uh, I don't, um . . ." Moreno stuttered, then smiled. "You're messing with me."

"Yes, and I'll try to watch the lecturing. Now let's see what my detectives have found out."

"What we got, Alice?" Blevins asked the lieutenant sitting at a computer with two screens. She was in her mid-fifties, nearly Blevins's age.

"Dr. Peter J. Boykin, thirty-nine years old, Anthropology Department at the University of West Florida. Grew up in northern California. Ph.D. in paleoanthropology from Stanford. He's hunted the Bigfoot all around the Pacific Northwest, the rougarou in Louisiana, even went to the Himalayas to look for the yeti. Here's his blog about his expeditions." She pulled up the website on one of the screens.

"A real true believer, huh?"

"Yeah. He claims to have all kinds of proof. He posts pictures of plaster casts supposedly of giant footprints and dark figures that he says are the creature, but they just look like shadows to me. He's had hair samples analyzed, well, he analyzed them himself, and says they're of no known species."

"Sounds no different from stuff all those other Bigfoot hunters say. Anything distinctive at all?"

"Take a look at this." Lieutenant Jacobs scrolled down the page. "Right here. 'The scientific community will never take seriously my work nor that of others in the field until a sasquatch body is produced. My intention, then, is to kill one, despite the objections from most of my fellow cryptozoologists. We can then study the specimen and have the DNA sequence to compare with the many samples of material taken by me and other researchers.'"

"Is that legal?" Moreno asked.

"Most states have a bag limit of one per season," Blevins said. "Same as for unicorns and dragons."

"You're messing with me again, Major," Moreno said.

"Dewitt brought in the guy's rifle," Jacobs said. "It'd been shot recently. Had an infrared scope."

"Boykin mention what he'd been shooting at?" Blevins asked.

"He hadn't posted on his blog for a few days," she said. "His last updates talk about hair and droppings. One line about hearing howls at night."

"Anything about people he ran into here? Rangers? Locals? Starlights?"

"Not a word."

"How about email?"

Jacobs took off her glasses and rubbed her eyes. "I've been through some. He was corresponding with a couple of other cryptozoologists, one in Oregon and another in Vancouver. Ordinary things like he found some evidence and about how hot it was."

"Anyone notify his family?" Blevins asked.

"Doesn't appear to have one. I called UWF and talked to his department chair. Said Boykin was well liked by all of his colleagues, even though they all thought he was nuts. Students loved him. No known enemies, except that a year or so ago he engaged in a debate with a local minister about evolution and got a few nasty calls and emails from religious fanatics that nobody took seriously."

"Thanks, Alice. Let me know if you run across something." Blevins turned to leave with Moreno at his heels.

"Blevins," Jacobs said. "Have you, uh . . . ." She looked at Moreno.

"I'll wait for you in the hall, Major," Moreno said.

When Moreno was out of sight, Jacobs said, "I just wanted to tell you that I think it's great that you're out working a case. Good way to get your mind off, you know, other things."

"Thanks."

"I mean, it's been two years."

"You're a good friend, Alice. I appreciate it."

"Anything about Diana?"

"No."

Jacobs stood and looked Blevins in the eye. "She's a tough, smart girl. I'm sure she's OK. You have to believe that."

"I try."

★★★★★ ★★★★★ ★★★★★

Detective Haynes sat in a room of eight desks where other members of the Major Crimes Division filled out paperwork, made phone calls, and drank many cups of coffee. Blevins was greeted by all with nods and good afternoons when he entered.

"What you got, Caleb?" Blevins asked.

"I've been skimming these journals a little bit," Haynes said. "Not much help. He chronicles his hikes through the woods, samples he collected, what not."

"Anything about people he talked to?"

"Just says the rangers have been friendly but skeptical. He did mention seeing somebody in the woods at night. Says he got excited when he saw what appeared to be a biped, and when he put the infrared scope on it, it was a girl. Looked like she had a long stick in her hand. She must have seen him, too, because she ran off."

"Wonder if that stick could have been a bow."

"Those scopes don't give enough detail, just shapes of heat releasing objects. I wouldn't think that he could even tell if it was male or female."

Blevins took a small bottle of pills from his pocket and washed one down with coffee. "Does he say anything about talking with Mingo Mauser?"

"No, but I haven't read it all."

"OK. Keep at it. Where's Kurt?"

"He was just here. Can't be far."

"I need him to . . . ." Blevins saw Detective Dewitt enter the room and met him before Dewitt could sit at his desk. "Kurt, I need you to go out to the fire tower. See if Ranger Renfroe can remember where Boykin placed his cameras and ask him to take you to them. Collect them and bring them back here."

"Major," Haynes said. "Boykin's journal has satellite coordinates for his camera traps."

"Excellent," Blevins said. "We're able to track those, right?"

"Should be," Dewitt said. "Alice can check his computer for the software he used and then download it for me."

"Good," Blevins said. "You've still got a few hours before dark. And take Moreno with you. I've got some desk work to do."

Blevins went to his office and closed the door. He pulled a bottle of bourbon from under the false bottom of a desk drawer and had a slow draw. He replaced the bottle and leaned back in his chair. The pill began to take effect. Blevins took a deep breath and held it for as long as he could as he had been taught. Practice had got him to nearly a minute and a half. The buildup of carbon dioxide increased the calming sensation that was replacing the anxiety. Blevins preferred the term "angst" that was so popular during his days as a philosophy student, but he knew that anxiety had a chemical cause while angst is a necessary condition of human existence. Perhaps, he thought, he should once and for all defer to medicine instead of Kierkegaard. Sickness unto neurotransmitters instead of sickness unto death.

Blevins was startled when his phone rang. He ignored it and arose from his desk, went out to his car, and drove home.

★ ★ ★ ★ ★ ★ ★ ★ ★ ★ ★ ★ ★ ★ ★ ★

Dr. Somers thumbed through a folder of notes and charts. "Nearly two years. Would you say things have improved?"

"Changed," Blevins said. "I'm not sure about improved."

"What's changed?"

Blevins crossed his legs. The leather chair squeaked under him. "For most of that time I struggled with guilt. I wanted to convince myself that I was justified, but I knew I wasn't. I think I'm better off accepting responsibility, embrace it as part of my essential being."

"Are you referring to your wife's death or losing touch with your daughter?"

Blevins uncrossed his legs, leaned forward, and looked at the footstool in front of him. The upholstery's paisley pattern reminded him of the arabesque designs he'd seen in pictures of the inner walls of mosques. "Both. I can't separate them. I'm responsible for both."

Somers wrote in the folder. "Is this part of your existentialist view of life? Last time you were saying something about Sartre and bad faith."

"Maybe we could call it an identity crisis. Who was that, Adler?"

"Erikson."

"If I can identify myself as wife killer and daughter—what?— estranger? That's not a real word I suppose. I may as well say daughter killer, too. I'm the cause of her running away, which I guess is a kind of symbolic killing."

"I'm not sure that locking yourself into an identity is helpful, especially such a negative one," Somers said. "Didn't Sartre emphasize personal freedom? I think he called it transcendence. You're always free to reshape yourself."

"It might be my way of putting it to rest, you know, sort of like this is what I am, now I'm done with it."

"Sounds more like rearranging puzzle pieces and calling it finished even though nothing fits."

Blevins had a sip of coffee. Somers roasted and ground his own coffee beans that he had shipped to him green from Ethiopia. It was always extra strong, unlike the bland stuff at the Sheriff's Department. "I don't know. I just thought it might be a different cognitive strategy, one I could at least get a grip on."

"I want to talk about your moods before we run out of time," Somers said. "How about your depression? Any improvement there?"

Blevins leaned back and looked at the clock on the bookshelf. How candid did he want to be? "Ups and downs. I'm taking the lead on a homicide case, hands on, playing detective out in the field instead of directing things from the office. Might distract me."

Somers wrote more notes in the folder. "Good idea. Is it working?"

"Too early to tell. I have to admit it may be the first thing I've enjoyed in two years."

"That's promising. Some patients respond to a change of habit or a change of scenery more than meds. You're on Wellbutrin now, 300 milligrams, and Klonopin, one milligram. You've been stable, right? Any dangerous thoughts?"

Here it is, Blevins thought. Do I tell the truth? Why else am I here? "Funny. Thinking about suicide gives me a certain comfort. Puts me in control. I don't *have* to live. That freedom—the ultimate freedom. The ultimate choice."

"'Ultimate' is certainly the right word. You haven't reported any suicidal thoughts in some time. Let's see." Somers thumbed through pages of notes. "Four months ago. I'd hoped we were out of the woods on that. How frequent?"

"I don't know, maybe daily. I don't dwell on it. More like a daydream for a minute or two until it calms me. Then I holster my pistol and get back to whatever I was doing."

"Wait—what was that?"

Shit, Blevins thought. How could I have let that slip out? Somers is going to think it was some sort of unconscious cry for help. "It's just part of the exercise. Obviously that's how I'd do it, I mean, that's part of the daydream. I really haven't been close to carrying it out. Like I said, it makes me feel in charge, that's all."

"What triggers . . ." Somers paused and smile. "Excuse me. Bad choice of words. Any pattern to when these thoughts arise? Any common features, time of day, activity?"

"Evening, at home. I'm too busy at work. Maybe just sitting there alone in the same house where everything happened."

"Are you always armed?"

"Well, not now," Blevins said. "Don't worry—no clean up here today." He laughed. Somers did not. "Everyone at the department is always armed."

"Would it be a good idea for you to turn in your gun for a while? That's allowed, isn't it?"

"I suppose so. Allowed, that is. I don't think it's necessary."

"Do you have your own guns at home?"

"No." Blevins lied. He owned five pistols—two Walthers, two Glocks, and a Sig Sauer—and a Beretta shotgun his wife bought him for their tenth wedding anniversary. Everyone he knew in law enforcement was a gun lover.

Somers tapped his pen on arm of his chair. "I'm inclined to think that giving up your gun is important, at least for now. This 'exercise,' as you call it, is too risky. Next thing you know you might cock the hammer . . . is it a revolver?"

"No."

"So it has a clip. Always have a round in the barrel?"

"Of course."

"Then the next step in your exercise might be to push the safety off. Then you might put just a little pressure on the trigger, like playing chicken with yourself."

Blevins had done exactly those things. He wondered if Somers was testing him, looking for a sign—a twitch of the eyelids, a tremor in the lips—that Blevins had played this chicken game. "I get you. OK then. The Sheriff probably won't like it, and he'll give me some sort of pep talk about how I can 'man up,' but OK."

"Maybe I should give him a call today, tell him it's medically necessary."

"You don't need to do that," Blevins said. "He'll understand."

Somers leaned towards Blevins and spoke in a softer but lower voice. "Listen, Blevins. I don't need to remind you that I have the authority to have you institutionalized, and if things appear to me to turn sour, I will not hesitate to do so.

"No. I mean, no, you don't have to remind me."

"Okay." Somers picked up a pocket calendar from the coffee table between the two chairs. "Instead of our usual monthly sessions, I want to see you again next week. Looks like all I have is Monday morning at eleven, just four days from now. How's that? Double check with Kristina, and she'll call you early on Monday to remind you."

"Sure," Blevins said. "See you then. Thanks."

When he got to his car, Blevins unlocked the door, lifted his holster from the seat, and removed the pistol. It had been sitting in the sun and was as warm as flesh.

FEBRUARY 2016

The Florida Sheriffs' Symposium in Tallahassee was the most boring conference Blevins had ever attended. He knew that if he won the upcoming election he would have to attend these kinds of affairs several times a year, probably the worst drawback of being sheriff. He'd asked Sheriff Humpy Baker if he could attend, and Baker, on the verge of retirement, was happy to let Blevins go in his stead. "Want to see what you might be getting into, eh, Bombardi?" Baker had said. "Can't say I'm going to miss those damn things. But you might actually learn a thing or two of value if you're elected. Maybe some new technology Lord knows we could use around here."

The second day of the conference was nearly over. Blevins had found nothing worthwhile in the presentations he had seen. The overcooked chicken breast and under-seasoned yellow rice of the luncheon had done nothing to settle his sour stomach from the bottle of bourbon he'd finished in the hotel room the night before. No one would miss him if he left early. His wife and daughter were not expecting him home for another day, so it would be a nice surprise to be home for Valentine's Day. The department is usually rather quiet at night. He could stop by and catch up on some work.

Blevins got back to Ocala at 8:30 PM after stopping at Pappy's Pit near Gainesville for a fried gator tail sandwich and buying a bottle of bourbon at the liquor store next door and a large, heart-shaped box of chocolates and a card at the grocery store across the street. At the department he was greeted by only a couple of colleagues. Things were slow, just as he had hoped. As he filled out a stack of forms that had doubled in size while he was away, he wondered why all of it could not be electronic. So much time could be saved without these paper forms that, when completed, had to be photocopied and filed in three different offices. He checked his watch—12:10. Where had the time gone?

He said goodbye to two people on his way out and got to his car. He tried the ignition, and the engine turned over but would not crank. He tried twice more and gave up. As he was approaching the door of the building, Sergeant Chip Dalton exited. "Hey, Blevins. What you doing here tonight?"

"I was just catching up and trying to head home, but my vehicle won't start."

"Need a jump?"

"No. Turns over but won't catch."

"Flooded?"

"Flooded? How old a car you drive? Listen, can you run me by the house? I'll have my wife bring me back in the morning and get Cole to look at it then."

Sue's Prius was in the driveway beside Blevins's Ford F250, and no lights were on in the house when Dalton dropped Blevins off at the curb. Sue and their daughter Diana were surely upstairs asleep. Blevins entered quietly, and was greeted by their Airedale terrier.

"Hey, Apollo," Blevins said. He squatted and rubbed the dog's ears. "Why aren't you up in bed with Diana?"

Blevins left his boots by the door, sat on the couch with the dog curled beside him, and turned on the television. He kept the sound low and scrolled through the cable movie channels. *Cool Hand Luke*, his favorite film, had just started. Blevins could watch for a few minutes, have a couple of glasses of the bourbon he had bought earlier, then creep upstairs to slide into bed beside Sue. He wondered if she would be frightened when she awoke in the morning and felt him there. Perhaps if she found him on the couch after she was fully wake she would not be startled. He was more tired than he thought he would be. His eyelids began to sag.

He was awakened by a noise in the kitchen, perhaps the backdoor closing. Then he heard a man's voice. Blevins rolled off the couch. He drew his .45 from the holster on the coffee table and pushed off the safety. In the murk of sleep or drunkenness, he moved through the den in a crouch, the pistol leading the way. As he got to the kitchen door, the light came on. A man said, "Fuck."

Blevins fired twice.

Sue crumpled to the floor like a dropped marionette.

★ ★ ★ ★ ★ ★ ★ ★ ★ ★ ★ ★ ★ ★ ★

Tiny copper women in hula skirts and yellow leis danced on the bright pink silk of the state attorney's tie. Blevins hoped it had been a gift. Would any man pick out such a thing for himself?

"You've been with the Marion County Sheriff's Department for twenty five years, Major Bombardi. Is that correct?" the attorney asked.

"Twenty six."

"You've probably had a great deal of training with firearms and been placed in training scenarios in which you had to decide whether or not to fire, right?"

"Yes."

"According to your department's records, you are not only an excellent marksman but you also score very high on those quick-thinking sorts of tests. Correct?"

"I do OK." Blevins had known Charlie Haskell for years. Haskell had prosecuted a number of men that Blevins had arrested.

"Then your wife's death was—what?—some sort of anomaly in which all your training simply vanished for that one instant and you fired your weapon in your own home without knowing who or what you were shooting at?"

"Objection, Your Honor!" Blevins's attorney called.

"Sustained," said Judge Martin. "Mr. Haskell, I'll tolerate no more inflammatory questions from you."

"I apologize, Your Honor," the state attorney said. "Now, Major Bombardi, can you please remind us why you returned home early from the conference in Tallahassee?"

Blevins popped his jaw as if blowing a smoke ring. His left ear was so congested that he could hear nothing from it. He had to turn his right ear toward the attorney and wondered if the jury thought he was purposely looking away from his interrogator. He thought he recognized several jurors' faces, despite Haskell's successful arguments to dismiss nine prospective jurors during the voir dire examination claiming them to be too closely acquainted with the defendant. Blevins's own lawyer had raised questions about six, saying that they had publicly endorsed the Mayor in the previous election, but the judge dismissed only three. "As I said, the conference seemed a waste of time. I came back a day early and stopped by the department to catch up on some work."

"And you had no idea that your wife was having an affair with Mayor Todd and had been for nearly a year?"

Blevins could hear Sue's voice, wafting across the kitchen table late one night, telling him that his suspicions were ridiculous. The content of her words was less important than the form. When serious and measured, she seemed to speak in meter, classical and alluring. On that night, it was mostly anapest, two short and apical syllables followed by a sonorous and beguiling long one, dah dah DAAH, dah dah DAAH, no afFAIR, no one ELSE, all the while pointing at him with the index finger—two short joints than a long one—by which he was taught in college to use as a reminder of that meter. When emphatic, she rapped her purple nails on the table in spondee, two longs—TAP TAP. All of this, it sounded, was spoken in italics, the dark sounds from her lyre-shaped lips leaning and curved.

The other senses would join in. The longer Blevins looked at Sue, the more her features would take on the shapes of vegetables. Her eyes turned into the star shapes of cross-cut okra when she was sexually inviting. Her nose turned like a crooked neck squash. Then smells, like a sliced, fresh tomato, especially any time she was tender and needed him to hold and whisper soft words to her. When angry but a bit guilty, like a banana pepper just snapped in half.

"Major?" said Haskell.

"I'm sorry. No. I had no idea."

"So, it's not possible, not possible at all you say, that you knew of the affair?"

"Your Honor," Blevins's lawyer said. "The question has been asked and answered already."

"Mr. Haskell," the Judge said.

"Yes, Your Honor," Haskell said. "I just wanted to give the accused a chance to clarify. Now, Major Bombardi, you've admitted to drinking earlier that night, correct?"

"Yes."

"And the same is true of the night before that, isn't that right?"

"Yes."

"I'm sure that as a law enforcement officer you've seen people do things under the influence of alcohol that they wouldn't normally do. Sometimes a man may hold a grudge or harbor a fantasy for months or even years and then one day, or night, he's had a few too many and gets a little full of himself, a little carried away, and comes up with a scheme. You've probably arrested a few people under such circumstances, haven't you?"

"Your Honor," Blevins's attorney said, "does my client have to answer that question?"

"No, he does not," the judge said. "Mr. Haskell, I'm getting impatient."

"Sorry, Your Honor. Major Bombardi, you testified that you did not unload your service revolver when you arrived home and that it had lain on a coffee table, loaded, for over an hour, correct?"

"Yes."

"Is that unusual, or do you often have a loaded weapon in the den with you?"

"I sometimes unload it immediately, sometimes a little later."

"I see," Haskell said. "Now, you also testified that you fired your weapon, the one that had been lying there loaded this whole time," Haskell looked towards the jury, "with the kitchen light on. Wouldn't that mean that you could see your victim, excuse me, your target?"

"I testified that I fired *as* the light came on. I believed that my wife and daughter were upstairs and I feared for their safety, so—"

"And you fired your weapon twice, correct?"

"Yes. That's how we're trained. It's called a double tap."

"What happened after your wife was hit by the bullet and she collapsed?"

"I dialed 911 and requested an ambulance."

"Mayor, I should say, former Mayor Farris Todd has testified that you held your gun on him for a moment before making the call."

"I don't remember. Perhaps. It may have been instinct."

Haskell placed his hands into his suit jacket pockets and pursed his lips. "Would that have been an instinct developed through training, the same training that should have prevented you from shooting your wife? Wouldn't that training have told you to shoot Farris Todd, too? You might as well had—you sure killed his political career."

"Your Honor!" yelled Blevins's attorney.

"Counsel in my chambers at once!" said the judge.

★ ★ ★ ★ ★ | ★ ★ ★ ★ ★ | ★ ★ ★ ★ ★

Sheriff Baker held a small, chrome Jesus on a crucifix and flicked back the thorny crown with his thumb. A blue flame emerged from Jesus' head to light the Sheriff's Cuesta Rey cigar. "I never doubted you'd be found innocent, Bombardi, but it must feel good to have it over with."

"Yes."

"Here's where things are now. I understand why you pulled out of the race. Now even though Todd's brother has been disgraced by this whole thing, Todd is going to continue his run for sheriff. I doubt anyone will oppose him. Damn thing's a shame in every way. I'm satisfied you'd've won, and you'd've been one hell of a sheriff. We all step on our dick sometimes, you know?"

Blevins looked at the framed photo of a younger Humpy Baker shaking hands with and being given a plaque from former Florida Governor Bob Martinez. Blevins remembered years before when he'd buy the *Miami Herald* just to read humorist Dave Barry's column in which Barry liked to say that Governor Martinez "is *NOT* a vampire."

"Yes, Sir. I guess the longer it is, the more we step on it."

Sheriff Baker laughed. "I reckon so. Now, I'm putting you on a month's leave, with pay. The department will also pay for you to see a shrink during that time, and I don't want to hear any lip from you about that. You can pick the shrink if you want to, but there ain't but a few in town. This guy Dr. Somers is supposed to be pretty good. That's who Murphy saw last year after his fiasco. Seems to have helped him a heap. Hell, I'm not sure if I was supposed to mention that. You know, privacy and all. If the shrink says you need more time off or more counseling after you come back, we might be able to pay for more."

Blevins stood. "Thank you, Sir. I'll see the shrink, and I'll be back in less than a month."

After six months, which included four months of unpaid leave, Blevins returned to the department.

FEBRUARY 2018

At 6:30 AM, Blevins entered the department and was stopped at the front desk by Sergeant Evans. "Major, there's a woman in lock up that Haynes said you should talk to. Forest woman, Melissa Hill, been picked up a couple of times for prostitution. Shot a guy in the leg last night."

"I remember her," Blevins said. "Shot her husband a couple years back, didn't she?"

"That's her. Did some time for it."

"So why do I need to talk to her?"

"Mentioned your homicide," she said. "Might be nothing."

"Let me get some coffee first," Blevins said.

The woman sat on a cot alone in the cell. She wore cut off jeans and western-style boots with silver tips.

"Ms. Hill?" Blevins said, "I'm Major Bombardi."

"I know who you are." She pulled back her wavy blond hair, brown at the roots, and tied it back with a rubber band. "You were in the paper."

Blevins entered the cell and sat on the cot opposite hers. "Can I get you some coffee?"

"No. They give me a cup. Tasted like mud hole water."

"You're right. I guess I'm just used to it. Now, what brings you here today?"

"I done told the deputy about this bullshit. If more men were gentlemen these days, they wouldn't have to be taught a lesson. I just made sure Jack Hampton learnt his."

"This Hampton is who you shot?"

"Just in the leg. He'll get over it."

"Let's go over the story," Blevins said.

"It'd be a whole lot easier if I had a smoke. You got one on you?"

"I'm sorry, no."

She pulled her feet onto the bed and leaned back against the concrete block wall. "No matter. So I'm stopping off at the gas station at Nuby's Corner for a pack of smokes and here's Jack talking to the guy who owns it. I don't know his name, but I've been knowing Jack for years. Lives just down the road. Used to be friends with my husband and just as sorry."

"This is the husband you shot in the leg years ago, right?" Blevins asked.

"Looks I got a habit, eh?" She laughed. "Anyhows, Jack's saying about this guy camping out there who's hunting the skunk ape. I say I hope he finds it and kills the damn thing. You ever seen it?"

"No."

"Well I have, and tell Jack and the other guy. They say I'm full of shit. I tell them about the thing coming up to my trailer about a year ago and peeking in the kitchen window when I'm fixing tuna helper then trying to get in the door. My dog Abbie starts to barking—she's just a little runt my friend Dot give me—and I guess that's what scared it off. Left a hell of a damn stink though. Whew! You'd think a pack of skunks had been fucking out there." She held her hands before her face and examined her orange fingernails. "I used to like to sit out in the yard at night and listen to the frogs and the night birds but I been afraid to since then."

Blevins finished his coffee. "And you shot Hampton because he ridiculed you, Ms Hill?"

"Everybody calls me Spinner. Anyhows, hell no. I just tell them to kiss my royal rump and pay for my smokes and go out to the car. Jack comes running out, saying he didn't mean to hurt my feelings. That's when he propositions me."

"For sex?"

"Said he wants to fuck me up the ass. That's the way he says it—*up* the ass, not *in*. That just flies all over me, him talking like that and me a lady. Then he offers me fifty-five dollars, says that was all the cash he had on him, and that I can drive his car. He's got an old Mustang convertible. I've always liked that car. Hell, put a couple of Bud Lites in me and let me tool around in the Mustang a while and I probably'd give him a blow job just so. Any respectable man ought to know that. By the by, any chance a blow job might get me out of here?"

"Afraid not."

"Can't hurt to ask, right?" She extended her leg and nudged Blevins's shin with the toe of her boot. "Anyhows, so I'm driving his car and he's talking about the shit he's been up to like fishing and race cars and mud bogging and all I can do is think about how my old man used to talk that same shit all the time and me telling him that he loved all them things more than he loved me. It was like Jack was talking and all I could hear was my old man's voice and see his face on Jack. So I says I'm turning around and going back to get my car and go home. He gets the red ass right fast, just like my old man used to do any time I'd say I's going to do something on my own. You sure you ain't got no cigarette on you?"

Blevins patted his pockets as if he were searching. "Nope. Are you saying you shot Hampton because he reminded you of your ex-husband?"

"Not ex. We still married, he's just—what do they call it?—estranged. Funny nobody never uses that word excepting with married people that's left. If your dog run off, wouldn't nobody call it your estranged dog, ain't that right? But I felt kind of bad for shooting Jack. I mean, it ain't like I love him."

"I don't understand."

Spinner leaned from the wall and crossed her legs under her as in a meditation position. "When I told my old man that he didn't really love me, he says that I didn't love him neither. I say I damn well did, and he says prove it. So I shot him in the leg."

"That's how you proved your love for your husband?"

"It takes some serious dedication to watch someone you love suffer. It was just a little .25, so I knew he'd be OK. I reckon if I'd've loved him more I would've gut shot him." She laughed and slapped the top of her boot. "Anyhows, I'm feeling bad that I shot Jack in the leg with the same pistol. Seems like a insult to my old man. I guess I still love that bastard. He give me that .25 for an anniversary present. Kind of fitting for me to shoot him with it, ain't that right? You of all people ought to understand about what somebody might do for love."

Blevins took the tiny plastic bag from his shirt pocket and swallowed a Lexapro. He rarely needed one in the morning.

"That's something I can't do," Spinner said. "Take a pill without nothing to drink. No sir. Gag me to death. That for nerves? Looked like a nerve pill. Anyhows, about the time we get back to Nuby's Corner, Jack puts his hand on my tit. So I just reach into my purse and pull out my little .25—I got a permit for it—and shoot him in the thigh. I hate to think I might've ruined that leather seat. It's one fine ride."

"Ms. Hill, Spinner, I'm not really here about the shooting, but I appreciate your honesty. The skunk ape guy was found dead at his camp. Now, did Hampton say anything else about him?"

"Dead? Ain't that some shit. Jack said the guy was asking around to find people who'd seen that monster. He was stopping people in the Winn Dixie parking lot after church. There's a church right there by Winn Dixie where Hammy's Pawn Shop used to be. Caught Jack and Mingo there. You know Mingo, right? Now there's a piece of work if there ever was one. Anyhows, Jack said there weren't no such monster and Mingo got the red ass over that. Said there's demons all out in them woods and that scientist guy didn't know what he was messing with."

"Did they get in a fight about it?"

"I don't think nobody hit nobody, but sounded like it must've been a big fuss. That Mingo's got a bad temper. I can't stand to be around him. The preacher come out of the church, I think his name's Cantrell, and got Mingo calmed down but not before Mingo said something about the wrath of God soon going to be on them."

"Did Jack take it that Mingo was threatening the skunk ape hunter?"

Spinner shifted on the cot to hang her legs off the side. "Hell, I don't know. I wasn't but halfway listening to him. Didn't sound like too interesting a story to me. Just more men's bullshit. About that time I turn the car around and head back. Damn what a sweet ride."

Blevins stood and handed her his card. "I appreciate it, Spinner. If you remember anything else, give me call, hear?"

She turned the card over between her fingers as if looking inspecting a gemstone. "OK. Say, see if you can't find me smoke, will you, hon? And when I get out of here, I'll return the favor. What you drive?"

▰▰▰▰ ▰▰▰▰ ▰▰▰▰

Blevins sent Detective Haynes to the hospital to interview Jack Hampton and took Moreno to the Forest to talk to locals. They stopped at Rabbit's Auto Repairs and spoke with Rabbit and two mechanics. Either they knew nothing or were unwilling to say. The same was true of three other Forest residents interviewed at their homes and the employees of the Forest Boat Center. Blevins had the suspicion that they all had heard of Boykin's death but wanted no involvement.

Blevins and Moreno went to Krazy Karla's Kitchen for an early lunch. Only the four old guys were in the restaurant.

"Look who's back," said Fedora. "Must be something pretty hot been going on out here, huh, Blevins?"

"It's hot, all right," Nasty said. "Weather man said this morning it's going to be in the mid-nineties. Probably already is. Hotter than a two-peckered bat up a witch's ass."

"Wait," Fedora said. "Witch's ass supposed to be being cold. Ain't you never heard people say it's colder than a witch's cooter on a brass broom? Oh. Pardon me, Ma'am."

"That's because of the broom," Nasty said. "The brass is what makes it cold, you stupid bastard. You think she sits on a cold broom all day? Like I say, it's a hot one, ain't it Blevins?"

Blevins and Moreno sat at a table beside the old men. "That's for damn sure," Blevins said. "Look, I was wondering if you old philosophers could help me out. I could use any information I can get on this skunk ape chaser. Anything at all. Y'all know anybody he talked to? A store he stopped at?"

"You're pissing in the wind, son," Beard said. "You know how tight-lipped every damn body out here is. My money's on one of them Starlights. They all a bunch of queers, you know."

"What you got against queers?" Cigar asked.

"Bunch of goddamn cornholers," Beard said.

Cigar pointed at Beard with his chewed cigar. "Ain't a thing in this world wrong with cornholing. Don't tell me you ain't never done it."

"With a man or a woman?"

"I ain't the one questioning nobody's sexual—how they say it?—preference. I'm just saying you can't say you ain't never done it with some damn body some damn where."

"Maybe I'll give you that," Beard said. "But them queers suck peckers, too."

"Nothing wrong with that neither," Cigar said. "They's a whole lot of people might suck a pecker, but that don't mean they queer. Ain't that right, Karla?"

Karla had just entered the room from the kitchen. "Now that's enough of that ugly talk. Can you believe these old coots, Blevins? I bet this young lady deputy here never heard the beat in her life. Ha!"

"I'm sure she hasn't, Karla," Blevins said. "I believe I'll have the grilled chicken sandwich today. Onion rings."

"Same for me," Moreno said, "except no onion rings. Just the sandwich. And no mayo."

"Oh, I don't put mayo on it, darling," Karla said. "Got my own honey mustard sauce with a tad bit of Datil peppers straight from St. Augustine."

"Sounds good," Moreno said.

"Now that's a pair if I ever been seeing one," Fedora pointed to the small television on the shelf beside the handwritten sign that said "No Profanity." "That's that TV preacher with old Zim Bob. Wonder what all they been being in cahoots about."

"I seen them on the news this morning," Nasty said. "That's Reverend Possible Pyron. Ain't that a name for you? He's got a brother some-where up the country name of Necessary. Ain't that some shit? Anyhow, this here Pyron said this storm is God's punishment for Florida for not using the Lord's resources as He meant for them to be used. You know they saying that storm might turn into a hurricane? You believe that, in February? Know what else? Evi-damn-dently this Pyron's having some tent revivals down here."

Cigar laughed. "Now there's the shit in a tent y'all were talking about the other day!"

Moreno leaned across the table. "Who's Zim Bob?"

"Robert Way," Blevins said. "One of our fine senators we sent to Washington. Extremely conservative, religious zealot. He used to go to Africa on church missions. Bob Way. Somebody added Zim, like the country, Zimbabwe."

"Clever," Moreno said.

"One of his main pushes is to privatize all state and federally owned lands. That would mean the Silver River State Park, the National Forest, all of them. I wonder why this televangelist is teaming up with him. Probably just more of the religious right's anti-government notions."

"Hot damn!" Fedora said. "We done be making the national news."

The Fox News anchor reported on the dead bears. Stock camera footage showed a grizzly raiding a trash can. The anchor said that authorities are baffled but suggested that "the incidents may be in retaliation for the five people killed by bears in the past year."

"That's the most shittingest ass lie I ever heard!" Nasty said. "Ain't nobody never been killed by no bear around here, and that's the most gospelest truth. They can't even show a picture of the right kind of bear. We got black bears here. That was one of them grizzlies like they got up in goddamnit Alaska."

"I hope they kill every last one of them," Beard said. "Bear killed my coon dog."

"Since when you ever coon hunted?" Cigar asked.

"I ain't never did. I bought that dog from a coon. Old Bunky Staples, worked for Woodrow Gaskins. They called him Amtrak because he walked real fast."

"Red Jesus," Cigar said. "First you carrying on about the queers, now you got to be racist, too."

"I ain't *got* to be a damn thing, except white," Beard said. "And that don't make me racist. For your information, I ain't never judged a man," he glanced toward Moreno, "or woman, for the color of their skin in my whole sorry ass life. I just like the old ways of talking before everybody got so picky about it. 'Coon' is a old-time word. Don't mean nothing hateful at all, so I like it."

Cigar stabbed his soggy stogie into the air. "Offensive is the kind of word it is."

"It don't offend me." Beard slurped his coffee and turned to Moreno. "How about you, miss? It offend you?"

Moreno opened a pack of saltine crackers from the plastic bowl on the table. "Well, sir, yeah, it does, I guess," She put the two crackers into her mouth.

"Told you," Cigar said.

"Speaking of them bears," Fedora said. "Blevins, I was running into Mingo Mauser this morning at the bait shop."

"What you buying bait for?" Nasty asked.

"I wa'n't. I was getting a co-cola and a pack of crackers. Is it any of your business where I take my breakfast? Like I was trying to say, Mingo goes to asking me if I'm wanting to buy some fresh bear meat. Saying it'll put lead in my pencil."

"You ought to've boughten forty pound, then," Nasty said. "I bet that old pencil of yourn ain't writ nothing in years." Beard and Cigar fell into whips of guffaws.

"I already know about it," Blevins said. "Mingo, that is, not your pencil." More laughter from the old men. "The Game Commission will burn him for that. We'll find whoever's killing them."

"Hell," Nasty said, "they ain't nothing but them old hog bears."

"How you mean hog bears?" Fedora asked.

"No bigger than a hog," Nasty said.

"So it's OK to kill little bears, but it'd be a bad thing if they was bigger?" Fedora asked.

Nasty sipped his coffee. "If they was bigger, then they wouldn't be hog bears, now would they? I swear to goddamnit God, you so damn ignorant I ought to jack slap you."

"What in the hell is jack slap?" Fedora asked.

"You don't want to find out.

"How about them monkeys on the river?" Cigar asked. "I hear they're catching arrows too."

"I hate them old ugly things," Beard said. "Back when I was a glass-bottom boat pilot at the Springs—"

"Here we go," Nasty said.

"—when the boats were still running," Beard said, "them

damn monkeys would squat up in the trees right by the water and throw shit at you."

"You hating about everything today," Cigar said.

"You ever get shit thrown at you?" Beard asked.

"From you right now," Cigar said.

"That Silver River ain't hardly much of a river at all," Nasty said. "The St. Johns, now that's a river what's worth a good goddamn."

"I'm going to be regretting asking this," Fedora said, "but what's so great about the St. Johns?"

"It's the onliest river in the whole wide world what flows north," Nasty said.

"What about the Nile over there in Africa?" Fedora asked.

"Don't count."

"Why not?"

"Crosses the equators. Once it crosses the equators, then the directions swap." Nasty tipped his cap at Fedora.

"That's the most dumb assedest thing I ever heard. And there ain't but one equator."

Nasty sipped his coffee. "Don't blame me 'cause you don't understand science."

Karla placed two Styrofoam cups of tea on the table for Blevins and Moreno, then refilled the old guy's coffee cups. Nasty had his own ceramic mug shaped like a pair of breasts.

"If that storm turns into a hurricane and heads this way," Karla said, "I'm leaving for my daughter's place up in Georgia. I sure ain't trying to ride it out like the last time."

"You talking back in aught four," Nasty said. "We're a long time overdue. Maybe that preacher's right. Why else would we have one in February unless the old man upstairs had something out for us?"

"Since when you been being so superstitious?" Fedora asked.

"Since when you can't see the shit writ on the wall?" Nasty said.

"Leave him alone, Elmore," Karla said. "I've told you about bad-mouthing the Lord."

The front door opened, and Mingo Mauser entered.

"Speaking of the devil," Fedora said. "Hear that, Karla? Maybe I been got a pinch of religion in me after all."

Mingo stood in the middle of the restaurant holding a large Styrofoam cooler and staring at Blevins. His eyes narrowed, and he worked his jaw from side to side as if trying to wear down his molars.

"How come you not on the water today?" Karla asked.

"I just need to see Lance for a minute," Mingo said. He walked into the kitchen.

No one at the tables spoke for a few seconds.

"Y'all's dinner ought to be ready," Karla said to Blevins and Moreno.

"Why don't you box them up to go, Karla," Blevins said. "We'll eat out on the road. Got a busy day."

"Don't we need to speak to this guy again, Major?" Moreno asked.

"Not here," Blevins said. "We'll catch up to him later."

Karla brought food in to-go boxes to Blevins and Moreno just as Mingo came out of the kitchen. His cooler dangled from one hand. It had obviously been emptied of its contents.

"Elmore," Mingo said, "I thought you kept better company than this." He tilted his head towards Blevins. From anyone else, Blevins thought, that would have been friendly needling.

Fedora smiled. "Better be watching it there, Mingo. That's a law man you be talking about."

"Law man my goddamn blistered ass. God bless y'all," Mingo said as he walked out the door.

"Wait here," Blevins told Moreno.

Lance turned from the refrigerator just as Blevins entered the kitchen. A spatula stuck out of his greasy apron pocket, and a cigarette jutted out from behind his ear under a backwards "Tooky's Lawn Care" cap. "Afternoon. What can I do you for, Mr. Bombardi, I mean, I guess, Deputy Sheriff?" He forced a smile.

"What did Mingo just bring you?"

"Mingo?" Lance squirted soap onto his hands and turned on the sink. "Let me just get this here chicken offen me." He washed his hands then rubbed them dry on his apron. "He brought me some deer meat he had in his freezer. He's generous like that since he got all churchy."

"You know you can't serve venison here."

"Oh no, no sir. That's just for me. Gonna take it home this evening."

"Bear neither."

Lance cupped a hand around his ear. "How's that?"

"Let me see it."

Lance opened the refrigerator door and stepped back. "Right there in them baggies."

Three gallon-sized zip bags held slabs of red meat that had been sliced into the size of rib eye steaks. Had the meat been left in large chunks, Blevins may have been able to identify it.

"I thought you said it came from his freezer," Blevins said. "This isn't frozen."

"Yes sir. It was." Lance said. He removed his cap and placed a hand on top of his head as if measuring his scalp. "He thawed it. Knew I'd be wanting to cook it up tonight. Me and Charlene loves us some deer meat. Mama, too. You ever had it in spaghetti? That's about the only way I can eat spaghetti."

Karla entered the kitchen. "Blevins, everything all right?"

"Yeah, Karla. I was just asking Lance if he was going to bring his fiddle to the Pickin' Shack. We didn't have a fiddle out there last week. Well, I'll see you."

Blevins and Moreno left the restaurant to find Mingo sitting in his idling truck. In the truck's side mirror, Blevins saw Mingo bite his lower lip as the truck scratched out of the parking area, flinging gravel against the department car.

★ ★ ★ ★ ★ ★ ★ ★ ★ ★ ★ ★

"She wouldn't give her name," Maggie said over the radio. "Insists on speaking to you and nobody else. I told her you were out on duty, and she said she'll wait all afternoon if she has to. At the Walmart in Silver Springs on 40. Just pull in, she said, and she'll come to you. I got her phone number, of course. You want it?"

"Negative," Blevins said. "We're coming back in anyway. I'll find her. Nothing much out here."

"And there's somebody waiting for you here, too. Strange little man. Said he was trying to find some missing people, your brother and his wife, best I can tell from his babbling. When he heard someone mention your name, he said he'll wait for you. He's in the lobby with a coloring book, mumbling to himself."

"Can't wait to meet him," Blevins said.

Fifteen minutes later Blevins circled the Walmart parking lot. At the end of a row of cars, away from the store, a woman stood under a Drake Elm. She wore an oversized, tie-dyed, peasant tunic and a wide-brimmed, floppy hat like women often wear in their gardens. As the car approach, she flicked up her palm from her hip. Blevins parked beside her and lowered his window.

"I'm Major Bombardi. You wanted to see me?"

The woman bent to see into the car. She looked at Moreno, then back at Blevins.

"Deputy, how about you go inside and get us a couple of cokes," Blevins said. "Would you like something, Ma'am?"

The woman shook her head. Blevins gave Moreno a five dollar bill.

"You serious?" Moreno asked. Blevins raised an eyebrow, and Moreno left the car.

The woman slid into Moreno's seat. Blevins recognized her to be a Starlight and judged her to be in her late twenties. Her teeth were yellow, and her sandaled feet were covered in white dust from the macadam road. The tattoo on her ankle of a face with round cheeks reminded Blevins of Zephyrus from Boticelli's *The Birth of Venus*.

"I'm Wind Walker," she said. "My regular name is Ruth. You showed me that photo of the girl."

"Yes," Blevins said. "Do you recognize her?"

"I think she's the dog dancer. Her hair is long, not short like in the picture."

"Is Dog Dancer at the camp now?"

"No, that's not her name. We call her that because that's what she does. She's an outlier."

A deputy's voice came over the radio. He had arrested two men for manufacturing methamphetamine. Blevins turned down the volume.

"I'm only telling you this," Wind Walker said, "because I think she's a runaway like I was. I'm leaving the Family, returning, as we say, to Babylon. Going home to Ashville and try to get my daughter back and start over. A couple years ago I wouldn't have said anything to you, just like all the others won't, but I'm older now and there's probably some parents somewhere missing her badly like I'm missing my little girl. Child Protective Services took her from me. I was on drugs, and the Family gave me support. At least I thought so then."

"What do you mean dog dancer is what she does?"

Wind Walker took off her hat and rolled it up as if she were about to swat a fly. "You've heard of horse whisperers? It's sort of like that. She holds a dog to her chest and moves around like she's dancing with it. Then she tells you things."

"What kinds of things?"

"Like if the dog is sick or worried, but also things about you. Animals can see into your soul, you know, and she can see what the dog sees."

"Does she sleep at the camp?"

She unrolled her hat and laid it upside down like a bowl upon her lap. "No. I'm not sure where she goes. I think I saw her about a year ago out west, and now she's here but not all the time. She was talking to that loud regular the other night when they found the dead beast chaser."

"Is she the one the regular and Ricky were fighting over?"

"Something like that. I was nearby talking to Vull and Sing the Fern about what we're going to do if that storm comes when I heard the dog dancer and the regular talking religion. They were getting loud, but I don't think they were angry. Ricky must've thought so, because he said something to the regular and then the regular chased him into the woods."

Blevins gave her his card. "Will you call me if you see her again?"

"I can try. It's hard to get a phone signal out there." She dropped the card into her hat and then flipped the hat onto her head. "Please don't tell anyone I talked to you."

"Of course not, but listen. Do you want to return home right away? I can help you with that."

"Thank you, but I can manage." She opened the car door and shifted to get out. She turned back to Blevins. "Can I ask you something? Is the dog dancer your daughter?"

Blevins cranked the car. "I appreciate your help."

Sergeant Evans waved her fingers toward herself to call Blevins and Moreno to the front desk as they entered the department. "That man over there has been waiting for you for hours," she said in a whisper. "We can't get much sense out of him. Crazy talk. I asked if he'd like to make an appointment for tomorrow, and he answered that he wasn't sick." She chuckled.

"OK. Tell Dewitt and Haynes I want to see them as soon as I'm done with this guy," Blevins said.

The man had a blue crayon in his mouth. He tore a sheet from the coloring book, wadded it into a ball, and placed it with other wadded sheets on the chair beside him. He had a crew cut and wore slip-on canvas shoes like those issued in jails.

"I'm Major Bombardi. How can I help you?"

The man jerked as if he'd been awakened. "Where's Tom at?"

"He doesn't live here. Why? Are you looking for him?"

The man removed the crayon from his lips and slid it into his T-shirt pocket with three other crayons. "I know they been here and living that time and then I didn't know but they weren't up home after."

"Let's go back to my office, Mister . . ."

"Purvis but don't nobody mister me and it's Driggers for a last name." He blinked his eyes rapidly three times as if they itched.

The name sounded somewhat familiar to Blevins. "Go see if Dewitt and Haynes found anything," he said to Moreno. "This way, Mr. Driggers."

Sergeant Evans buzzed open the door to the back, and Driggers shuffled after Blevins.

Blevins sat behind his desk. "Please, have a seat."

Purvis looked back and forth at the two empty chairs. He pressed his hand on the seat of one then the other. He chose the first one and settled in slowly as if he were afraid it might collapse under him.

"Tom Bombardi is my brother," Blevins said. "But he hasn't lived here for years. What do you need with him?"

"Ain't him really. He got Martha and I didn't mess with them but then when I was put away I just was thinking and thinking and just need her to come home with me back home. You the sheriff? Where they at? Go get her."

Blevins watched as Purvis opened his coloring book to a page with a duck that had been colored blue. The edge of the page was crimped as if it had been bitten. He judged Purvis to be in his forties. "Martha and Tom are married, Mr. Driggers, and have been for years. I doubt that she has any plans to leave her husband."

Purvis's head snapped up. His bloodshot eyes widened. "You doubt but don't know. I got the plans. She been thinking about me I know it. She ain't wanting him no more and now wanting to be mine and me hers and can take her to places. I got a truck."

"Mr. Driggers, you said you were put away. Was that in a hospital?"

Purvis shook his head. "Not a hospital where when you sick like them people and get shots. The Lieber Correctional. Ten years. They got sheriffs."

"Why were you in prison?"

"About me and Rembert growing that bad pot and them zombies in the shed and the sheriffs had to put me away but they let me out so I come down here. Martha couldn't come see me in the Leiber Correctional and I had to wait and nothing to do 'cept think about her and her purple hair. Let's go get her."

"Mr. Driggers, you have a place to stay here in town?"

Purvis took a green crayon from his shirt pocket, scratched off a bit from the rounded end with his thumbnail, then returned it to the pocket. "Yes sir sir I was sleeping last night a motel little place with a Hardees and orange-smelling beds and I was tired cause the driving. I wake up and drive the town and can't find Martha then seen this sheriff station and wanted help to find her."

"Can you wait right here for a minute?" Blevins stepped out of the office and saw Moreno across the hall talking with Dewitt. Blevins motioned for her to come.

"Yes Sir?"

"See this guy in my office? I'm about to get rid of him. I want you to follow him to see what he's up to. If he goes to his motel, just wait in the parking lot. Don't let him see you. I'll call you soon."

"Yes Sir. Is he a suspect?"

Blevins returned to his desk without answering Moreno. "I'm going to see what I can do, Mr. Driggers. The best thing for you to do is to return to your motel and wait to hear from me. OK?"

"OK yes sir sir." He stood up and put the coloring book under his arm and walked down the hall. Moreno saluted Blevins and followed Purvis.

Blevins picked up his desk phone. "Alice, see what you can find out about a Purvis Driggers. Did time at Lieber Correctional, which I believe is in South Carolina." He hung up the phone, closed his door, took his cell phone from his pants pocket, and pressed in a number.

"Hola."

"Hola yourself, hermano. How's our man in Havana?"

"Blevins? Well, I'll be petrified. Martha and I were just talking about you, how you ought to migrate down here," Tom said.

"Maybe that'll be my retirement home soon."

"It should be. It's got a ways to go yet, but the economy's growing at a surprising rate. Property's still cheap as communion wine."

"Well, I'll think about it," Blevins said.

"So, what's on your mind? You need a box of cigars or something?"

Blevins laughed. "No, I'll stick to a Cuesta Rey every now and then for the moment. Listen, this is going to sound odd, but when you left the monastery and you and Martha came down here, there was that guy after her up in South Carolina. What was his name?"

"Hmm. I seem to have a dim memory of an incident like that. After all, it was twenty years ago."

"Very funny."

"Purvis Driggers," Tom said. "Why?"

"I thought that was him. He's here in Ocala. He thought he could find y'all here and says he's come to take Martha from you. Wandered into the department to get help him in his, ah, mission, then heard my name and had to see me."

"Well, I'll be Saint Jude. After all this time. He went to prison years ago, drug charges, if I recall. I figured he was still locked up."

"We're running a check on him now. My best guess is—he's got the strangest way of talking, odd syntax—he obsessed on Martha while in the penitentiary."

"You think he's capable of violence? He never did anything violent while we were living up there. Even with all that mess with Martha, he acted more like a scared, desperate kid than a criminal. What are you going to do with him?"

"Legally, there's nothing I can do," Blevins said. "I suspect he'll give up soon and go back home."

"I'd keep a close eye on him if I were you."

"Yeah. He left my office a minute ago, and I sent a deputy to tail him."

"Maybe he'll step out of line, and you can pick him up and ship him back. Now listen. I'm serious, you know, about you moving to Cuba. I'll keep you busy with our organization. We can always use more volunteers."

"Well."

"You still have that old boat, right" Tom asked. "The Diana Two. When's the last time you took her out?"

"Two or three years ago. It's dry docked in Cedar Key right now."

"Martha and I still talk about the time the four of us took it all the way down to Marco Island. That's got to be over half way to Havana. You know it's a fisherman's dream down here. Hold on. Martha's waving at me." Tom paused. "She sends her love, says we got a bedroom waiting for you."

"Give her my love. I'll let you know what happens with this Driggers nut."

"You do that." Tom paused. "Blevins, still nothing on Diana?"

"No."

"You taught her to be strong. All that hunting and camping you did with her. Teaching her how to track animals. And was it aikido?"

"Jiu jitsu. You were aikido."

"Good enough. She can take care of herself. Keep the faith, brother."

"Sure." Blevins pressed "End" on his cell phone and took a Klonopin.

Detectives Dewitt and Haynes knocked at his door just as Blevins ended his phone call. He waved them in, and they sat in front of his desk. "What we got?" he asked.

"We've gone through his journals and digital voice recorder," Dewitt said. "Names a few locals he talked to about skunk ape sightings. Three claimed to have seen it and were at first eager to tell him about it, but then they each changed their mind and told him to leave them alone. Said he thought it has something to do with their religious beliefs."

"Does he mention Mingo Mauser?"

"Yes," Dewitt said. "Spoke to Mauser a couple of times. Odd. Says Mauser was very interested in the skunk ape and wanted to know all about what Boykin had found. Then he soured on it, and they had an argument."

"In a church parking lot?" Blevins asked.

"Yes, with the Hampton guy Caleb interviewed. Not clear what the argument was about, but a preacher, may have been Mauser's preacher, intervened."

"Obviously we need to interview this preacher," Blevins said. "His name might be Cantrell. What did you get from Hampton, Caleb?"

"This guy near about talked my ear off," Haynes said. "He thought I wanted to know about him getting shot and just carried on and on about that 'crazy skank bitch' who shot him after he was 'just trying to be friendly.' Said he told Boykin that the skunk ape was just uneducated rednecks' imagination and an educated man like Boykin should know better. Hampton said he himself was educated, graduated from the College here. Took a couple of philosophy courses, so he can recognize horse shit when it's dressed up and served on a plate. He told Mauser that his religious ideas about demons were just as foolish, which set Mauser off and he threatened both Boykin and Hampton."

"What sort of threat?" Blevins asked.

"Well, Mauser didn't exactly say he'd do anything," Haynes said. "Something about the wrath of God striking them like lightening. Hampton said he just laughed at Mauser, and

Mauser bowed up like he was fixing to pop Hampton. That's when the preacher came over and cooled them down."

"OK," Blevins said. "What else? Did you get those cameras?"

"Yes Sir," Dewitt said. "Not much on them so far. A few pictures of deer, a bear, one cool one of an owl flying right in front of the camera with a mouse or something in its claws. A couple with something in the background that we can't make out. I'm sure Boykin would have sworn they were skunk apes."

"Probably so," Blevins said. "Give me the names of those people Boykin mentioned. You two go see Mauser first thing in the morning. First dirt road past Buck Head Bridge. Green house at the end. He's a fishing guide and usually heads out pretty early. I'd go see him myself again, but he's not going to tell me anything. Be sure to go together. He might get a little testy. I'm going back to see the Starlights now."

"We'll let Moreno know," Haynes said.

"No. I don't need her," Blevins said. "Close the door behind you."

The detectives left, and Blevins reached for the bourbon in his desk. He took a swallow and began to think back to his days in graduate school. Had he finished his Ph.D., he'd now be looking back at a long career as an academic. He would probably have written a few books, one on Kierkegaard, another on Heidegger, maybe one on Jaspers. He might have landed a position, perhaps an endowed chair, at a prestigious university in a great city and been invited to international conferences where symposia would be held to discuss his groundbreaking work. He and Sue could have spent their summers in Paris and Vienna. Diana could have traveled the world and been the envy of all her friends. They could have learned Mandarin or Hindi together. How could he have been so stupid? One moment of weakness, one slip of intellectual integrity, and it all vanished.

He finished the bourbon and put the empty bottle into his briefcase. He would go home and change into plain clothes and drive his own car into the Forest to speak with the Starlights. Perhaps when he passed around the picture this time, they might be more willing to take a closer look. On the way out he would buy another bottle of bourbon. No, scotch instead. Sometimes change is good.

MARCH 1990

After two hours in the bus station, Mingo had gone through thirty-one pages of *Awaken the Buddha Within* and five beers. Each time he bought a Budweiser, Crump, who was more lurking behind than working the counter, gave Mingo a smirk. They had worked together for eight years at All Nation Trucking, but Mingo had the suspicion that Crump considered him just another of the growing number of unemployed men who spent most of the day at the station when they had been passed over in the morning at the work pick-up across the street. "Us black men gonna be the end of you crackers," Crump liked to say back at All Nation. "We got styyyyle. Yah-ha!" Six weeks into the strike, Mingo knew that if something did not give soon, he would be standing there at 6 AM, too, hoping for nothing more than to spend the day at the business end of a Mexican backhoe. Could a little style save him?

Mingo worried that the pages of the book, the first he had picked up in years, would slice his softening fingers, and that he was getting too old to absorb new knowledge. A paper cut might be the only mark the book would leave on him. What a sorry state, he thought, to be thirty years old with tender hands and a callused mind.

A bus pulled in, and the passengers boiled out. A rangy bald guy with a duffel bag across his back entered the station and stopped in front of Mingo.

"Namaste, asshole," Mingo said.

Bud did a slight bow and put his palms together for an instant, more like a clap than a reverential gesture. "Namaste. Peace of the lotus to you."

"I'll take a big piece. I'm sitting here starving."

Bud adjusted his duffel bag strap across his long-tailed, collarless shirt.

"My first advice to you," Mingo said, "is to shed those sandals and let's stop at Wal-Mart for a pair of skips and a Metallica T-shirt or something. You're going to get your ass kicked just for looking like that. Hell, I might do it myself."

Bud showed no reaction. "We can go now." He smiled with an expanse of mouth and unchanged eyes. Shaving nicks dotted his scalp.

★ ★ ★ ★ ★ ★ ★ ★ ★ ★ ★ ★ ★ ★

"I can't believe this old contraption is still running." Bud hadn't deposited his duffle bag into the back of the truck but instead held it to his chest as if he thought something might fall out. He seemed more relaxed now. "I thought you'd chauffeur me in the Old Man's Caddy. You know, a little style for the returning first born."

"What do you know about style?," Mingo asked. "Riding the dog. Planes cost about the same."

"I need to be close to the earth." Bud fished in his bag and withdrew two filterless cigarettes. He did a fancy trick flip of a Zippo and lit the cigarettes as the lighter rolled across his fingers like a chip in an edgy but adept poker player's hand. He spat a bit of loose tobacco out the window and handed a lit cigarette to Mingo.

"I didn't know you Buddhists smoked," Mingo said. "I thought y'all ate rice and sipped tea all day." The smoke tasted peppery.

Bud held the cigarette to his nose and stared at it as if searching for a defect. "Tea is just dried leaves. What's tobacco?"

"Not the same."

"Everything's the same."

"Bullshit."

Bud took a long drag and crossed his eyes to watch the smoke seep from his nose. "The Heart Sutra says form is emptiness, and emptiness is form. The two do not differ. Same is true of feelings, perceptions, thoughts, consciousness."

"Then Cadillac or International Harvester. Should be the same difference to you."

Bud was motionless, still focused on the tip of his nose.

"The Old Man's at the lake with the Caddy," Mingo said. "He uses it to fish with since he went on disability. Did you even know about his accident?"

Bud snapped out of his micro-meditation. "Fish with?"

"You'll see. Or would that be an image you can't perceive, that whole form and emptiness deal?"

Bud spied the book on the seat between them. "Are you curious about Buddhism?"

"I've been in the library every day for two weeks researching, trying to figure out what would bring you back. I didn't come up with an answer. So, why are you back?"

Bud flipped the Zippo through his fingers again and it lit and snuffed out all in an elegant whirl. "Master Fong, my master, told me I had to seek peace."

"Peace? Here? I think I get the form-emptiness joke now."

★ ★ ★ ★ ★　★ ★ ★ ★ ★　★ ★ ★ ★ ★

They parked near the lake and walked through the sand to the water. Bud produced a telescoping walking stick from his bag and looked like he was measuring his paces. Every few steps he kicked a sandaled foot out behind himself like a fastidious cat.

They stopped twenty yards from the Cadillac to observe. The Old Man, their father, couldn't walk since the front end loader tilted over onto his hip, so he sat in the car in the passenger's side with his left arm and leg stretched to drive like an old fashioned rural mailman. He sped in reverse for about five yards and hit the brake. The jolt, he claimed, added spring to his cast out the window with his right arm.

"He can't do that from the truck?" Bud asked.

"No air conditioner."

The driver's side window lowered. "I see you," the Old Man said. "Best not be waiting for me to come to you."

Mingo and Bud approached the Caddy and were about to lean into the window when the Old Man hit reverse. The lure arced over the water and splashed by something bobbing, maybe a boat cushion. He eased the car toward the water and retrieved the slack in the line.

"Who's the skinhead you got with you, son?" the Old Man asked. "Looks familiar, but just seems to escape me." He reeled in the lure, giving it a sideways jerk with each revolution of the baitcaster Diawa. "Wait, I believe that's my very flesh, hairless and cane-walking. You got a bad hip, too, Bud? Bud the Buddhist. Buddha Bud. Hey, Bud Bud!" He squalled in laughter. "How about that, Mingo? Let's call him Bud Bud."

The Cadillac hit reverse again, and Bud and Mingo jumped back. The lure flew out, the car eased up, and they remained a step away from the driver's side window.

The Old Man adjusted the passenger side mirror so that he could access their reflection while he kept a squinted eye on his lure. "What's all that paraphernalia you got hitched up to you there, Bud Bud? Look like a junk man sporting his wares."

Bud's duffel sagged from his back, and assorted adornments hung from his waist (a wooden bowl, a wooden ladle, a shaving brush all bundled together; a tiny drum on a handle like the Cherokees sell up in the mountains, a wand in a sheath), his shoulder (a book on a leather lanyard, three little burlap sacks with drawstrings), and his neck (a whistle, a beaded necklace with a medallion that looked like a puzzle).

"Ah baby!" The Old Man yanked the rod. "She's a-rooting, boys!" He played the fish a while and then reeled it right across the dirt and up to his window. He giggled and snorted as he pulled the lure from the bass's mouth. "Come around here and look at her, boys. Not a bad one."

The Old Man hefted the bass by the jaw. He had ropy arms and amply veined hands that looked like they itched to grab a torque wrench. "She's four pounds sure enough. Still good plate size." He reached down and opened a cooler just under the window. Three fish and a pint bottle of Ancient Age lay on a bag of ice. He deposited the fresh bass and withdrew the bottle. He took four sips—one for each pound as was his custom. The bass looked to Mingo no more than two pounds.

"What's hanging in that sheath, Bud Bud, some kind of

Jap gut sticker?" The Old Man pointed to what looked like a magician's wand.

Bud slid the little sword from its sheath and sliced a circle before him as if opening a hole in a curtain between him and the Old Man. He laid it vertically against his nose and assumed the cross-eyed gaze again. "This is my tanto. I am by training a sword master." He wiggled one of the burlap sacs. "Also tea master." He tootled on the whistle. "Flute master."

The Old Man hit reverse and went into his backswing. "Too bad you couldn't've been bass master." He cast, this one not so far. ""You might could've hooked old Jaws what's slunking around there."

"Not that shit," Mingo said. "The myth of the lake monster."

The Caddy made its way back. "Ain't no goddamn monster," the Old Man said. "You ever known me to buy that kind of superstitious shit? It's a catfish. Maybe a carp. Could be a giant eel. At least a hundred pounds. Eaten that Owens boy last year and Colby Harvey's Brittany gyp that he'd trained to retrieve *and* unhook his fish. Colby's probably out here somewhere in his wheelchair. That's what I need."

"You have a wheelchair," Mingo said.

"No, goddamnit! A dog for to retrieve my fish. Can't you course a conversation? Maybe Bud can, what with all that meditation they say them monks do he's been hanging around with. Brittanys are bird dogs, so that gyp could cradle a bream in its mouth like a quail, never even scrape off a scale." He yanked the reel, but missed whatever he thought had nibbled. "Anyway, that's how come you don't see any young'ns swimming out here, because of that whatever big ass fish is out there. What's your theory, Bud Bud?"

Bud whipped the little sword in a flourish and stepped about stiffly like in a military routine. "Rahula Bhadra, the Hymn to Perfect Wisdom, 'As the dew drops disappear in the sun's rays, so all theorizings vanish, once one has reached Thee.'" He slammed the sword into its sheath then hid his hand behind his back.

"Who's 'Thee'?" Mingo asked. "Perfect wisdom?"

"And you talk about me and *my* legends," the Old Man said.

"Perfect wisdom my numb ass." He hooked the lure onto a rod eyelet. "Here, Mingo. Stick this and the cooler in the trunk. Let's get on to the house and get your mama to fry up these fish."

Bud stared out at the lake as if awaiting a ship. His jaw muscles were clinched and his fist pressed into his thigh. A tiny stream of blood trickled from his hand down his leg.

Bud returned all his accessories to the duffel as he and Mingo walked to the truck.

"Find any of that peace yet?" Mingo asked.

Bud slung the duffel into the truck bed. "Maybe if you'd shut the fuck up."

★ ★ ★ ★ ★ ★ ★ ★ ★ ★ ★ ★ ★ ★

The family loaded food onto plates as Bud tried to tell about creating one's own hell. "Dukkha. Life is dukkha, craving, attachment, the root of all suffering. Like being attached to that recliner in there with a cold one then just wanting a bigger recliner and a bigger TV and more beer." He'd changed into Levi's and a salmon-colored T-shirt but some of his gear hung about him.

Sheila set a bowl of grits on the table. "It's vanity. The Bible says, 'Vanity of vanities, all is vanity.' Y'all boys want some hot peppers with your fish? Mildred give me a jar after prayer meeting last night. After all she's been through. Everybody in that house is out of work, but she puts up things from her garden and gives them away and just smiles like always."

"That's exactly the point," Bud said. He poured hot water from a small pot into his wooden bowl where he'd crumbled tea leaves from one of his miniature crocus sacks. He said the tea was from Siam. He whisked it around with a small brush. "The Bible prophets knew all about suffering. Vanity is the bastard child of the ego. The bigger the ego, the more dukkha, the more suffering."

"We sure learning plenty about suffering up in here," said Lizzie. She was Mingo's younger cousin who'd come back with a baby after a two-year stint as a carnie. Her parents wouldn't let her enter their house.

"Here's what you don't understand," the Old Man said. "Pass me them grits, Lizzie. Look here, Bud Bud—did I tell y'all that's his new name? Buddha Bud, Bud Bud." He snorted so loud Lizzie's child laughed and threw his sippy cup across the table. "You see, people here don't have time to think about that kind of shit. All they know is work from ashes to ashes and dust to dust. Do they suffer? Hell yeah, more than that Buddha of yours ever knew. Mingo told me about him. He was a damn prince living in a big fancy ass palace until he decided that was too tough for him." Sheila passed him the bowl of grits, and the Old Man spooned out a dollop onto his fried fish. "So then he wandered around the rest of his life eating other people's, *poor* people's, food. Never turned a lick in his rich boy life. Dukkha my gimped-up ass."

Bud spun his tea bowl around in his hands as if studying it for the first time. "That might be the major attachment around here then. Work. You're all slaves to work."

"There's some of that perfect wisdom for you," Mingo said.

Bud sipped his tea. "Are you trying to be ironic, you with your union? Do you make a move without the union telling you first?"

"You don't know what you're talking about."

"The Buddha said, 'Better to swallow a red-hot ball of iron than to live at others' expense while immoral and intemperate.'"

"Speaking of swallowing, did anybody say the blessing?" Lizzie asked. "We'd better get to eating before Bud Bud has us all wearing turbans around our heads."

The Old Man cackled. "Turbine, like a turbine engine? Ha! At least his head would have some moving parts then!"

"That's not Buddhists, goddamnit!" Bud dropped his bowl and stared at the spilled tea. His neck trembled, purplish-red as a rooster wattle.

"Can Buddhists take the Lord's name in vain?" Sheila asked. "*In vain*—that means vanity, don't it? I be dog. I never thought of that."

Bud went to the kitchen door, turned back to face the others, bowed with his prayer hands pointing at them, then walked out.

Sheila wiped her eyes with her apron. "Lord, he is a trial. Mingo, what's going on with him?"

"It's me, ain't it?" Lizzie asked. "He's mad about coming home and finding me and Peedro moved into his room. I knew this would be a problem. He never liked me."

The Old Man spit out a fish bone. "That's not it, Lizzie. He's just always been hard to get along with. Now I guess he just had to dukkha outside for a minute. Ha!"

Mingo went to the kitchen sink and looked out the window. Bud sat in the back yard cross-legged under a cedar, a cigarette hanging from his lip and a book spread across his lap. He tore out a page, touched it to the cigarette, and released the burning paper into the breeze. He did it again. And again. Mingo pulled the window curtains together and stood at the sink.

"Get on back to the table, Mingo," said the Old Man, "else I caught these fish *in vain*. Ha!"

★ ★ ★ ★ ★ ★ ★ ★ ★ ★ ★ ★ ★ ★ ★

"I'll get straight to it. I don't believe you went to any of those places," Mingo said.

Bud stared at the water rings on the bar top. He'd spent the week telling about the yeti skull he was shown in a Tibetan monastery that only the spiritually gifted are allowed to enter. He'd sipped tea from the skull and immediately had a vision of his past lives—kings and wise men and generals, no peasants or slaves or foot soldiers. In China he'd had a wife who ate only bamboo, like a panda. She was the only female member of an obscure sect on a mountain so remote that it had no name. They would sit and meditate facing each other in a cave of natural jade, and after one such session Bud came to and found her robe in a pile and her gone, either ascended to heaven like Elijah or, as Bud said, dispersed among the subtle universes. He'd studied sword mastery in Japan with a 140-year-old Zen master whose katana, upon command, would leave the ground and rise to its master's hand.

Mingo finished his beer and signaled to Cricket for another round. "When I totaled the years you say you spent in each place, you would have been gone about twelve years instead of four. What's more, some of your scriptural quotes don't sound right. You didn't take into account that I read up on this religion since you wrote that were coming home. And your parable about a possum? Not only did it not make any sense, but I don't think those nasty little rabid bastards live in India or China."

Bud listened, fingering the beads on his necklace like he was counting them. "I'm just seeking some goddamn peace. I thought I could find it if I left here, if I just got far enough away. 'Free everywhere, at odds with no one, and content with either this or that, enduring dangers unperturbed, fare lonely as rhinoceros.' It helped some."

"Rhinoceros? And far enough away from what? Here?"

"I thought so at first. This is a place of desperation."

"Where ain't?" Mingo took a cigarette from the little sack Bud had laid on the bar. "You either work yourself ragged and lie aching in bed every night worrying that that's all your sorry life will ever be, or you get laid off or go on strike and worry about *not* working. There's your sameness, anywhere you go." Stevie Ray Vaughan's guitar was stinging through a little stereo behind the bar, trading licks with somebody, maybe Albert King. "The blues. That's the one constant. Unless you're rich, and we damn sure ain't. I think the Old Man is right—Buddha never had the blues."

Crump and several others stumbled in together. They looked as if they'd started drinking much earlier. Crump was clean-shaven, his hair greased up into a shelf over his forehead, and all of the others were white. A redhead girl who looked familiar to Mingo was clutching the shoulder of Crump's burgundy suede jacket.

"There's different sorts of riches," Bud said. "Siddhartha's material luxuries meant nothing to him. Well, they meant something. Attachment. So he had to leave to nurture his spiritual riches. Leaving wasn't enough for me. So I studied. It helped some, too."

"So this is the famous monk brother, eh? Yah-ha!" Crump slapped Mingo on the back. "Cricket, bring us all a shot of

Crown, even my no-working friend Mingo here and his prophet brother." He whirled his hand in a circle over Mingo's and Bud's heads like he was tracing a boundary around them, lest Cricket might think he meant to buy liquor for the few other patrons in Pookey's Happy Time Joint, costing Crump another twenty bucks.

Crump rubbed Bud's head. "I remember when you had hair, buddy roe, and when Mangy, oops, I mean Mingo, had a real job hauling—what was it, hay, feed?—before he took up at that hell hole trucking place he just quit."

"Didn't you used to work there, too?" the redhead asked.

"I had the sense to get out of there two year ago," said Crump. "Damn wise decision, too. Now they been on strike for two months. Got to be tough, eh, Mingooooo?"

Cricket lined up eight shot glasses—Mingo, Bud, Crump, the redhead, and the blond, plus three additional men in Crump's contingent. Mingo doubted that the blond was of legal drinking age. The blond, who didn't seem to be paired to any of the men, was slack-jawed and missing a front tooth, and the three men all wore black, sleeveless T-shirts with crosses and hawks tattooed on their forearms. One had a cleft palate splitting the moustache that would have otherwise hid his entire mouth, and another had no eyebrows. The one who may have been intact had something oozing from an ear. The redhead smiled at Mingo. He wasn't sure if she winked at him or had an eye spasm.

The Crump coterie downed the shots and squeezed into a booth across the room.

"I don't really care what you believe," said Bud. "My enlightenment doesn't depend upon what you think you know or what you approve of." The Allman Brothers' "Wasted Words" played. Bud cocked his head as if he thought he heard his name. "This song says it all. See, wisdom comes if you're open to it."

The Crump conclave burst into laughter, the blond girl's high chirping rising above all. Mingo turned on the barstool to look at them. The redhead may have winked at him again.

Bud spun his empty shot glass like a top. "Master Pei taught me how to fashion sand gardens. He liked to spend an hour or so after sundown drawing foxes."

"How the hell did he do that? Cluck like a chicken?"

"What? No, dumbass, not *draw* like shit draws flies. *Draw* like with a pencil. Jesus, you used to be the smart one. That union brotherhood of labor has sapped the sense out of you. Master Pei used charcoal and drew foxes on rice paper in every position and attitude. So I finally asked him, 'Master, why are you so fond of foxes?' He answered, 'I am not fond of foxes.' 'But you draw them every day,' I said. 'Do they have some special meaning for you?' He looked at me with disappointment in his eyes, as if I had learned nothing from him, and said, 'I draw foxes because they are easy to draw. Long snout, pointy ears, bushy tail. Those are the essentials. The rest does not matter.'"

"Are you going to tell me the moral, or do I have to figure it out myself?" Mingo asked.

"You're wrong about the Buddha. He knew the blues better than anybody. He knew how to live *within* them, not despite them."

Another slap on Mingo's back. "Two more shots for these bums, Cricket," said Crump. "Are you letting these boys run a tab? God knows they don't have the jack to throw arooooound." Crump was wearing pointy loafers with silver caps on the toes. He leaned in close to Mingo. "I'm going to drain my crane, Mingo my man. Keep an eye on my Esther over there. Make sure one of them swags don't try to snake her, hear? Yah-ha!" He poked his thumb into Mingo's ribs and left for the hallway.

The name "Esther" called up a dim image in Mingo's head, a gauzy impression of a boat and a bikini-clad redhead. No sooner had Crump disappeared than Esther left her booth. Her eyes seemed to Mingo to look a curve around him, and she walked the same way, about ten degrees off plumb until she sashayed back on track. She stopped by bumping against him.

"Remember me, Mingo?" she asked.

"I think so. Did we go on a boat ride?"

She threw her head back to laugh and nearly pitched over. Mingo wrapped his arm around her waist to steady her. She smelled like bourbon and machine oil. When he tried to remove his arm, she grabbed his hand and pressed it to the small of her back. Cricket put two shots on the bar.

"You could say that," Esther said. "It was my cousin Hurley's boat. Well, my Uncle Wilbur's, really, but we were out in it and Hurley had his girlfriend Troxie. We were purrrty drunk. Didn't cramp your style none, though."

"I think I remember. That must have been ten or eleven years ago, huh?"

She moved her legs a few inches, and Mingo felt her lumbar muscles shift against his hand. He sat back straight and tried to slide his hand from her again even as he was trying to hatch a plot to get her away from Crump. She leaned in between him and Bud and then hiked her leg up to sit as if Bud weren't there. Bud moved to the next stool.

She glanced over Mingo's shoulder with at least one eye. "Here comes Billy. I'll bet he'll be tickled to know you and I are friends."

Mingo felt the blow to the back of his head and his face meeting the floor as if they occurred at once. He was dazed but without pain as stools clattered around him and Esther rolled onto her knees a few feet away. His ear was pressed to the floor and he could hear shoes scuffling. Esther was yelling "Billy! No! Billy!," and Mingo realized that he had never known Crump's first name. He saw the metal-capped shoes side by side before his face. One disappeared from his view, then something slammed twice onto his exposed ear.

The stomping ended, and the pain and ringing sound began. Mingo sat up and saw Crump curled under a table and gasping for breath as Esther sat on her heels in wild astonishment and the three guys scrambled from the booth. They knocked Blondie to the floor and charged the bar where Bud stood, slightly crouched, with his praying hands stretched out before him. He held something between his palms.

The moustached cleft palate got to Bud first. Bud swung his arms in semi-circles and the harelip crumpled to the floor. It looked to Mingo that Bud had hammered his fist down onto the top of the guy's head like punctuating a remark at a debate. Maybe Bud had hit him with the hilt of his little ninja knife. The eyebrowless one was next. Bud whirled to the side like a matador, kicked, and browless went back-peddling into a table. The third one swung a bar stool that caught Bud in the shoulder, knocking him over Crump to land on Mingo. Bud's medallion swung before Mingo's face. He saw that it wasn't a puzzle but a labyrinth, a crooked spiral to the center that doubled back to retrace the same route out to the entrance.

Crump caught his breath and kicked Bud in the shin. Mingo tried to stand, but Bud pushed him back down. Mingo saw blood and half of a broken liquor bottle on the floor. The ringing in his head diminished enough for him to hear Cricket slapping a baseball bat on the bar—she would often produce it from under the bar and make joking threats to customers—and yelling into the telephone and Blondie screaming "Esther, let's go!" and some other woman saying "Help somebody, Johnny!" and somebody, presumably Johnny, saying, "Ain't my damn business—we getting out of here!"

Mingo got his hand onto the bar and rose and tried to repel the dizziness. Cricket hollered that the law was on the way. One of the guys had Bud's necklace from behind and was choking him while another was trying to hit Bud, who was blocking each swing with his forearms. Mingo grabbed the bat from Cricket, and just as Harelip was about to stand, struck him on the head. It sounded just like the crack of a solid line drive.

At the rim of his vision Mingo saw Crump and then felt another blow to the head. He fell back against the bar as Crump took the bat and turned toward Bud. Two of the guys were down now, but one was still twisting the necklace.

Bud swung his hands behind him, hip level, and the guy screamed and fell. Crump brought the bat hard against the side of Bud's knee. Bud grimaced and slumped against the wall. The three guys and Crump made their way to him. They knelt before him, and all Mingo could see was a clump of backs and frantic elbows as they labored to get in punches.

The door opened and someone entered and appeared to Mingo to drop to one knee.

The men around Bud were all grunting and cussing and the motion slowed and the women stood nearby trying to see what was happening in the huddle.

"Fucking God," one man said. Harelip turned and vomited.

Blood ran from the top of his head. Esther and Blondie harmonized a low wail and scampered for the door. Crump turned toward Mingo as if he were trying to recall his face.

"Rhinoceros," said Crump, "He's talking about a fucking wandering rhinoceros."

The men hobbled out, grasping their respective wounds, passing by whoever knelt in front of the door. Bud sat against the wall, his hands on his chest, smiling.

Mingo stumbled to him, using a bar stool like a walker. He strained to focus his vision and to ignore the monstrous pain in his head. He sat in front of Bud, who looked as if he were hiding something in his hands. A trickle of blood seeped from beneath them. Mingo peeled back Bud's fingers. The hilt of the ninja dagger throbbed in Bud's chest. Mingo gripped it, not sure if he should pull it out or not. Mingo heard the person near the door move. He looked to see Deputy Blevins Bombardi getting to his feet, his eyes bulging, his mouth widening, his pistol dangling in his hand.

"I called the paramedics!" Cricket yelled from behind the bar. "Oh Jesus."

Bud pushed Mingo's hand away. "No," he groaned. "My last dukkha."

"Does it hurt?" Mingo felt foolish but didn't know what else to say. The knife looked like it was in Bud's heart.

Bud closed his eyes. "Not like it did before the blade went in."

Mingo turned to Bombardi. "What the fuck's wrong with you!" He charged the deputy. His shoulder slammed into Blevins's stomach, and the men fell to the floor.

"You let him die," Mingo grunted. He gripped Blevins's neck with one hand and tried to get the pistol with his other. He could hear Bud saying, "no, no, no," like a chant.

Two more deputies burst in. One flailed Mingo's broad back with a nightstick. The other guided the pistol, still held by Blevins and Mingo, to point at the ceiling. The first deputy landed a heavy blow to Mingo's head, and Mingo's limbs fell limp and his bowels loosened. The deputies rolled him off Blevins and onto his stomach and handcuffed him. Blevins holstered his pistol and told the other deputies that he was not hurt.

They lifted Mingo to his feet and leaned him against the bar. Mingo was dizzy and the bar sights swirled around him. He managed to focus his vision on Bud who still sat against the wall, still smiling.

Bud's head slid down to rest on his shoulder. He smiled and held out his bloody hands. "Look. The Buddha has awakened within."

FEBRUARY 2018

"You look a mess," Sheriff Todd said.

"Just need to catch up on a little sleep," Blevins said.

"Tell me about it. They upgraded that storm to a hurricane now. Looks like it's passing through on Valentine's Day. Lord knows I can't take any budget cuts now right when Eddie tells me we have to beef up Emergency Operations. Hear me? We'll have to prepare shelters for our own people plus those damn Starlights who probably don't have sense enough to get out of here in time. I've got a press conference coming up at noon. So tell me some good news about this homicide in the Forest."

"I wish I could. Nobody seems to know or is willing to say much."

"No suspects at all?"

Blevins cleared his throat. "He had an argument with Mingo Mauser."

"Not that son of a bitch again."

"Only thing we got so far. Mingo was also there when the body was found."

"Forensics?"

"The coroner confirmed the cause of death was a blow to the back of the head, but he can't say for sure what hit him. We found a good sized ball bearing near the body."

The Sheriff ate a Rolaids tablet. "Think somebody slung a ball bearing at him? Strange way to kill a man."

"Coroner said it's consistent with the wound, but if that's what did it, it'd have to be traveling in excess of 100 miles an hour."

"The Rays could use a pitcher like that. I want you to wrap this thing up quick. I hate it when the damn state moves in and acts like we don't know what we're doing. Well, today I guess

I'll just say we have some leads. Keep it vague. I'll try to steer the conversation to preparing for the hurricane. They named it Artemis. We've also got this TV preacher Pyron blowing into town. Wants to use the Silver Springs stage where they use to have all them music shows. He's trying to get the park to let people in for free. Expecting a thousand people to come hear him fire-and-brimstoning. So we'll have to provide security for that. Maybe the hurricane will blow them freaks away."

"Is that all, Ash?"

"I reckon so. Say, how's that kid Moreno doing?"

"She's a bright girl. Eager. I'll think she'll do fine."

"Good," Sheriff Todd said. "Maybe we can promote her quick, get that damn equity office off my back. Hear me? Too much on my plate, even for a big eater like me."

* * * * * * * * * * * * * * * *

Blevins sat at his desk and thought about something the Sheriff had said: *somebody slung a ball bearing.* He punched his cell phone.

"Hola."

"Me again, hermano."

"Two days in a row," Tom said. "You'd think we were kin or something. You're not calling to tell me Driggers is in a jon boat on the way to Cuba, are you?"

Blevins laughed. "Naw. My deputy said he went to his motel and just stayed there. I've got somebody on the way over there now to check on him again. Say, got a technical question for you. How fast can you hurl something from a sling?"

"A sling? Man, I haven't thought about that in years. You can throw something a whole lot faster than with your arm."

"I know that much. A hundred miles an hour?"

"Sure, someone who's practiced at it a while. I never got as accurate with it as I wanted to. Better with a bow. But Diana, now she could whip that thing like all get out. Hit a bull's eye at thirty yards. She was as good a slinger as she was an archer. Why do you ask?"

"Just a hunch," Blevins said. "We have a homicide out in the Forest. Has a wound in the back of the head, and we found a half-pound ball bearing nearby."

"That could do it. You might just have a modern-day King David on your hands. Back in the ancient world slingers were as important as archers in battle."

"That's helpful. Thanks."

"OK. Now the important thing is you need to get your ass down here."

"Well."

"We'll have a Cuba librè chilling for you."

"Well. Never can tell."

★ ★ ★ ★ ★ ★ ★ ★ ★ ★ ★ ★ ★ ★

"His truck was nowhere in the parking lot," Moreno said. "I asked the motel manager, and he said he hadn't checked out. What's up with this guy, Major?"

"Just seems a little disturbed," Blevins said. "Looking for some people he thinks live here. Probably nothing. Let's head back out to the Starlight camp."

A Sheriff's Department car was parked near the Starlights' Great Door when Blevins and Moreno arrived. Tock and two other barefoot young men meet them at the gate.

"You about to pitch a tent here, Leo?" Tock asked. "Last night and again this morning. I think we could call this harassment."

Blevins glanced to see Moreno's puzzled face.

"Just following up," Blevins said. Twenty yards away he could see Wind Walker. She ducked behind a tent. "We're going back out to the beast hunter's campsite, give everybody here a chance to wake up."

"You won't find much," one of the other Starlights said. He had a bandana tied around his head and a small padlock through his earlobe. "The other leos took everything. Two of them are out there now."

"I know," Blevins said.

The yellow tape still encircled the clearing. Haynes and Dewitt stood by the fire ring.

"One last look?" Blevins asked.

"We were out this way anyway," Dewitt said. "Thought it couldn't hurt to sniff around again."

"If I may, gentlemen," Moreno said. "Now the body was lying here with his head in that direction, and his back was this way, right? So if someone threw something at him, it would have come from that way, away from the Starlight camp."

"Wow, Deputy," Haynes said. "We would have never thought of that."

"Better not make fun of her, Haynes," Dewitt said. "The kid might be our boss someday."

"Y'all talk to Mauser?" Blevins asked.

"Yes Sir," Dewitt said. "Two game wardens were already there, and Mauser was none too happy with them. They fined him a thousand dollars, and he insisted that they couldn't do that if he didn't have the bears. They said that a law enforcement officer's report was all they needed. Mauser kept yelling 'Habeas corpus! Habeas corpus!'

"Kurt and I couldn't keep from snickering," Haynes said. "Then Mauser stuck out his hand and spread out his four fingers with his thumb tucked under to point at all of us, like he was putting a whammy on us, and started hollering about the wrath of God."

"I take it that the interview was useless then, huh?" Blevins asked.

"Yeah," Dewitt said. "We tried to question him when the game wardens left, but he just babbled."

"I think he was speaking in tongues like the Episcopals do," Haynes said.

"That's the Pentecostals," Moreno said. "The technical term is glossolalia."

"You hear that, Detective Haynes?" Dewitt said. "The deputy must've been to college. She's going to be our boss sure enough."

"You reckon we ought to start saluting her now?" Haynes asked.

"OK, OK," Blevins said. "Was another man there with him, named Shaky, I think?"

"No Sir, but Caleb saw a girl," Dewitt said.

"She stepped out of the shed then ducked right back in when she spotted us," Haynes said. "She must've thought that we'd left the same time the game wardens did."

"Did you get a good look at her?" Blevins asked.

"Not really. Young, maybe her twenties. I just assumed it was his daughter."

Blevins swatted a mosquito on his arm. "Well, I guess we're pretty much done here. How about that preacher?"

"On the way now," Dewitt said.

The detectives left. Blevins heard the car crank and drive away. He walked around the perimeter of the campsite, inspecting the bark on the pines and stooping to look under ferns and palmettos, despite little hope of finding anything. Moreno followed, examining the same things Blevins did.

Blevins stopped to look at the center of the clearing where the tent had been. "We might as well—"

A *tunk* sounded nearby. Two feet from Blevins an arrow trembled in a pine tree.

Moreno fell to the ground and pulled out her pistol. "Get down, Major!"

"No need. That was a warning shot."

"Should we pursue?" Moreno was panting.

"No. Whoever shot that arrow knows his way around here a whole lot better than we do, and I'm too old for chasing somebody through the woods. Let's go to the ranger station. Smart money says that this is the same type of arrow used on those bears."

Blevins wriggled the arrow from the tree trunk. It had a bleeder tip, the kind used for big game, not for target practice.

"Major, shouldn't you be careful, you know, in case there's a print?" Moreno stood and brushed pine needles and dirt from the front of her uniform.

"Not a chance. This archer would have thought of that."

Back at the car, Blevins tossed the arrow into the back seat.

"Major," Moreno said. "I think it's that guy's truck."

Two hundred yards down the road sat an old Isuzu Pup.

"Let's go see what he wants," Blevins said.

As they slid into the car, the Isuzu did a three point turn and drove in the other direction. Blevins got his car turned around.

"You think he followed us, Sir? Why would he do that?"

"This guy's probably delusional. I think he's harmless, but we can't rule out that he has some bizarre scheme. He believes that I can take him to people he's tracking."

The truck sped up to fifty. Blevins raced through the white cloud of macadam dust and turned on his siren. The truck slowed and stopped on the grassy edge.

Blevins walked to the driver's window. The tread was nearly all worn off the truck's tires, and the left side of the back bumper was bent down about twenty degrees. Moreno positioned herself at the back right of the truck as she'd been trained and unsnapped the thumb break on her holster.

"Mr. Driggers," Blevins said. "I'm surprised to see you out here. Did you follow me?"

Purvis leaned his head out of the window. He wore the same plain, red T-shirt he had the day before. The crayons were still in his pocket. "You in back. Following got to be in the back and not in the front. You following."

"I mean earlier. Did you follow me out here?"

"You was on this road then I was on this road and we here on this road now."

"Mr. Driggers, let me be clear. Martha and Tom live in another country. I think you should go back home. OK?" Blevins saw two empty Milwaukee's Best cans on the passenger seat.

Purvis took an asthma inhaler from the ashtray and squirted albuterol into his lungs. He held his breath a few seconds, then exhaled. "Cordesville, South Carolina. My home is that. This is Florida."

"Right, and they are not in Florida. You're wasting your time here."

"It's the morning time. The Lieber Correctional time I been wasting. That Tom. He run her from me. Then they come back and I was being nice. Then I do the time in the Leiber. Ain't got no time for wasting no more."

Blevins thought about locking up this nut for a night. Perhaps that would scare him enough to get rid of him. "I want you to listen closely, Driggers. Leave Ocala before you get into trouble. Go back to your home. There's nothing and no one for you here. You don't want to get locked up do you?"

Purvis shook his head. "No no sir." He looked into the rearview mirror as Moreno moved around beside Blevins.

"Major, should we search this vehicle, check for a bow behind the seat?"

"I highly doubt it, but let's take a look," Blevins said. "Can you step out of the truck, Mr. Driggers?"

"Yes, sir. I know good how to step outen a truck. You done been telling me to leave."

"You can leave in a minute. Now come on out." Blevins opened the door and Purvis slid out. "Just stand right there by the bed."

Blevins leaned the seat up. Two rolls of toilet paper, a 2011 calendar from a pawn shop in Charleston, S.C., and a Stanley Phillips head screwdriver. Moreno opened the passenger door and looked in the glove box.

"This vehicle is twenty-five years old. Registered to DeWayne Driggers. It expired in 2015," Moreno said. The box also contained maps of Georgia and Florida.

"DeWayne that's my brother," Purvis said.

"Driving with an expired registration is a serious crime, Driggers," Blevins said. "Now, unless you want me to lock you up for that you need to go back home right now."

Purvis got into the truck and drove away without a word.

"What a peculiar person," Moreno said. "He must have some mental problems. Did you notice how he fidgeted?"

"Oh, he's got problems, but they're not ours. I believe we've seen the last of him. When we get back in, call that motel just to make sure he checked out."

★★★★★ ★★★★★ ★★★★★

"That's the same kind of arrow all right," Ranger Fleming said. "I guess whoever's doing this can face an attempted murder charge now, huh? That thing would probably go right through you. That's how they did with most of those monkeys. I talked to Toby Tillis at Silver Springs this morning. You know they found about two dozen dead? A few had the arrows still in them but most the arrow passed through them. Picked up the arrows yards away. One monkey had the arrow through its neck and was pinned to a cypress. Game Commission's sending some wardens to help out. Going to lay up in them woods and try to catch somebody."

"I can send a few deputies," Blevins said.

"I durn well appreciate that. Maybe this hurricane will chase off whoever it is. Hurricane Artemis. Greek goddess of the hunt. Kind of fitting, isn't it? Shooting a monkey in a tree is one thing, but you got to be an experienced woodsman to get a bear, especially that many. And you got to be fairly close with a bow."

"We've never had this kind of thing, bears killed and just left there, have we?"

"The poachers we've had always take the carcass and sell parts overseas. Mostly Korea and Japan. Impotent old bastards think the bile's like Viagra. You can get ten-thousand dollars just for a bear gall bladder on the black market. Paws, too."

"Any ideas why somebody'd do this?"

Fleming got up from his desk and adjusted the thermostat. "You know this month has been hotter than last August? We finally got rid of those window units and got central air. I reckon we'll put her to the test now." He sat down and tapped his index finger on the desk. "Well, I got a theory. It might be crazy, but wonder if those Cain brothers aren't behind this. You know those billionaires who fund all those republican politicians? They pumped some money behind Zim Bob. Every congressman who's sponsored bills to sell government land to private industry is backed by Cain money. Happening all out west. They're getting some fierce opposition from the EPA and groups like the Sierra Club, but how can you fight that kind of money?"

"I thought those guys were mostly after oil," Blevins said. "They want to drill everywhere and build pipelines. What would they want here?"

Fleming pointed at Blevins. "Remember that hunting lodge in Texas the governor caught flack about going there? This would be an ideal place for something like that. All those politicians bought and payed for by those billionaire Cains would start coming here instead of Texas. I think the governor and Zim Bob would think that would make Florida even more powerful. You see that Reverend Pyron who's going to preach at Silver Springs? Zim Bob's coming too. That won't be a sermon about saving your soul. If they get rid of the bears and the monkeys, they'll clear out the nuisances. They've been lying about them. I heard Pyron on the news talking about all these people who've been killed by bears when there's been absolutely zero, and he said the monkeys spread AIDS. Said that Marion County has the highest rate of AIDS in the nation. You watch. When Pyron's done here, visits to Silver Springs and out here will plummet. You'll have every Republican in Florida screaming that this land should be sold off."

"I hope you're wrong, Mickey," Blevins said. "I hope it's just some wacko and not something so . . . sinister and pervasive. I appreciate your help. Say, you going to make it out to the Pickin' Shack Saturday night? Moreno, Ranger Fleming is the best mandolin player in the county."

Fleming chuckled. "I don't know about all that. But I'll tell you, young lady, your boss here's a hell of a flatpicker. Makes that old Martin box ring like a greased bell. Now if he'd just quit trying to sing! Ha! I wish I could come out and pick one or two, but I'll probably be camped out trying to catch me a bear hunter."

★ ★ ★ ★ ★ ★ ★ ★ ★ ★ ★ ★ ★ ★

After speaking with more Forest residents and learning nothing, Blevins and Moreno returned to the department.

"So, what's a flatpicker, Major?" Moreno asked.

"Acoustic guitar player, uses a pick, a flatpick, instead of fingers. Someone who doesn't just strum rhythm but plays solos. You play any instruments?"

"No Sir."

"Well, why don't you come out with me Saturday night and listen? Generally there's a pretty good crowd sitting in lawn chairs and enjoying the music. Pretty informal. Beer and pot luck supper."

"Yeah. I could sit with all the other African Americans?"

Blevins laughed. "Serious, you'd be as welcome as anybody else."

"I'll think about it, Sir."

"OK then. Now you get ahold of that motel, and I'll see if the others found out any more than we did."

Lieutenant Jacobs was pulling her hair into a pony tail when Blevins got to her desk. "Afternoon, Alice. You get something on that Driggers fellow?"

"Yeah. Jesus, I can't believe this heat. Feels like the air conditioner's broke. Anyhow, ten years in the pen in South Carolina for drug manufacturing and human trafficking. He was working for another man who's serving a thirty-year term. They were growing some exotic sort of weed and had brought in people from Haiti whom they kept as slaves. I've never heard of this stuff, but it's toxic until it's hung up and dried, so they used these slaves to handle it. After it was processed, they sold most of it down here in Florida."

"That must be what he meant when he mentioned zombies to me, the slaves," Blevins said.

"Right. Apparently they kept these people imprisoned and drugged up the whole time."

"Anything about mental illness?"

"Saw a therapist the last year or so before his release. His cellmate complained that Driggers was acting paranoid and erratic. Whatever the diagnosis was, the shrink obviously thought he was well enough for release. You know how it is—I bet that system up there is as bad as ours when it comes to inmate psychological treatment."

"You're probably right." Blevins saw Haynes and Dewitt enter the detectives' room and sit at their desks. "Thanks, Alice."

Blevins crossed the room. Haynes and Dewitt had removed their ties and rolled up the sleeves of their sweat-soaked shirts. "You boys take a dip in the pool?"

"It's brutal out there," Dewitt said. "Why can't just one person we interview have air-conditioning in their trailers? I don't see how they stand it."

"I'll tell you what. Y'all can knock off an hour early today. Early start to the weekend."

"Thank you, Sir" the detectives said.

"Now, get anything?"

"It's like they're all in that old prisoner of war sitcom. What was it, with the sergeant who always said 'I know nothing, nothing'?" Haynes said.

"Hogan's Heroes," Blevins said.

"Yeah. You know how you can usually tell if somebody has something to hide? I'd say about half of them were like that. Right, Kurt?"

"Oh yeah," Dewitt said. "The only person who had anything to say was the preacher, Reverend Campbell it turns out, not Cantrell. Told us all about how the crypto was an evil man who was trying to undermine the 'truth of the word,' as he said. Said these scientists are trying to find the missing link and probably lying about it all. If the 'evolutionaries,' as he called them, can convince people that the missing link is in the Forest, then people will reject the Bible. He kept asking why we weren't doing something about these infidels."

"I guess he doesn't know how many so-called missing links we have," Blevins said. "The Australopithecines."

"Say what?" Dewitt asked.

"Our proto-human branch separated from other apes about six or seven million years ago. Then came the Australopithecines, then members of our genus, like Homo erectus, about two million years ago, leading up to Homo sapiens a couple of hundred thousand years ago."

"If you say so," Dewitt said. He looked at Haynes, and Blevins thought he may have rolled his eyes. "So, Campbell says that Perkins and Mauser and this other guy that we presume was Hampton were raising their voices while Campbell was shaking hands with his congregation after church. He went over to smooth things over. Says Mauser was just defending the word, but he knows that Mauser has a temper and was able to pull him away and kneel down with him to pray for the other men's souls."

"But he said that he can't delay the wrath of God," Haynes said. "Then he asked if we were Christians, and when we said we were, he made us kneel down and pray with him. Asked the Lord to bless us and to bless Reverend Pyron who will call down the angel of the Lord who will strike like lightning."

"I've been hearing that phrase a lot lately," Blevins said. "Did Campbell speak directly with Perkins?"

"No," Dewitt said. "Said Perkins went into Winn Dixie and he didn't see him after that."

"OK," Blevins said. "Now finish up here and hit the Ale House for happy hour. Don't be surprised if I join you."

★★★★★ ★★★★★ ★★★★★

The Famous Venus Mound Lounge, the largest of the myriad strip clubs in the Tampa Bay area, was packed, just like Blevins liked it. The unlikelihood that he would be recognized in Tampa was increased by the anonymity of blending in with a mass of drunks. He sat at the edge of a three-feet-high, circular stage that was surrounded by men awash in swirling, multi-colored lights and shelling out one-dollar bills and swigging overpriced, watered-down drinks. He politely rejected the women who sat beside him and said, "Want some company? How about you buy me a drink, Sugar?"

After an hour and a half of a variety of women of every ethnicity, some writhing and grinding—one was named Coffee, not because of her sepia skin, but because, as the an-nouncer said, "She grinds so fine!"—others taking to the pole for acrobatic feats with agility equal to that of a Cirque de Soleil performer, the emcee announced the appearance of Succulent Cicelia, the Belle of the Bay, whose olive skin and thick, black hair suggested a heritage from the Italian island whose name is a homonym for hers. Her routine was subtle with none of the gymnastics or mere undulations popular with the younger audience. Hers resembled a vintage burlesque with the elegant moves of an accomplished ballroom dancer and measured removal of long gloves and lacy garters. Fewer men tossed cash at her, but her older admirers rewarded her with more fives and tens than were slid into the other dancers' g-strings.

When she finished her routine, she circled the stage, and as she passed Blevins, she tilted her head toward the back of the club. Blevins followed.

The Royal Room was adorned with a red leather couch and

Chinese paper lanterns hanging from a ceiling that sported pink, Baroque cherubs surrounded by ribbons and roses. The walls in contrast featured large prints of naked women: a busty, boot-shod blond side-saddled with legs agape on a mechanical bull; an Asian woman in kabuki make-up stretched on a bed shaped like an enormous lily pad; an African-American woman in six-inch, white stilettos bending over to gaze back at the viewer through her knees, a martini glass balanced on her be-glittered buttocks.

Blevins sat on the couch as Cicelia disappeared behind a folding partition draped with plastic ivy. She emerged in a moment wearing a black satin robe that ended mid-thigh and plugged an MP3 player into speakers. Blevins recognized "Acknowledgement" from John Coltrane's *A Love Supreme* album.

"Missed you last week, Harry," Cicelia said. "Everything OK with you?"

"Just been a little busy. Didn't think I found someone new, did you?"

"Not you, Harry. You're a one-woman man." Her robe dropped to the floor and her arms rose above her head. She closed her eyes, swayed, and for two minutes said nothing, and to Blevins it was as if the entire world was composed of only a beautiful naked woman and a sublime saxophone.

"This may be the last time you see me, Harry," Cicelia said, her eyes still shut. "Time for me to retire. This is not the arena for a woman my age."

"Your age? You must be kidding. Those kids out there got nothing on you."

She turned her back to Blevins and continued to sway. "That's sweet of you, but it's time for a change. Besides, my daughter in Jacksonville split up with her husband. She could use my help with the kids."

"I'm sure there're places up there to dance. You don't want to waste your talent, do you?"

"Talent. Ha. I'll probably go back to teaching, You know I did that for five years before I found that I could make more money baring skin in front of a bunch of drunks? But that well is drying up. Not too many like you left who appreciate a classier act."

She turned back around, took her foot in her hand, and raised her leg high off the floor. "Not as easy to do this move anymore. These old tendons aren't as elastic as they once were." Blevins felt his pulse increase. "Come on, Cicelia. You can't be more than—what?—forty, forty-one?"

"Now, Harry." She released her foot, and her leg descended in a slow arc in front of her. "You know it's impolite to ask a lady about her age. But, hell, we're friends, right? I'm forty-six. It's only fair, since you've told me so much about yourself. You're a police officer, but not in Tampa, and you killed your wife a couple of years ago, and you suffer from depression." She closed her eyes again and chanted along with the voices from the speakers, "a love supreme, a love supreme." She moved a step closer to Blevins. "But you never told me your real name."

"Blevins."

"That's an uncommon name."

"It's a family name. Now you. What's yours?"

"Ophelia."

Blevins smiled. "Give my regards to Polonius."

She stopped moving and posed contrapposto, a subject worthy of Praxiteles, Blevins thought.

"Well, how about that?" Ophelia said. "A literary cop. My mother was an English professor, wrote a book on Shakespeare, but she died when I was a kid. I felt obligated to study Shakespeare as an homage to her. When other girls were singing New Kids on the Block, I was memorizing soliloquies. I recite them to myself when I'm on the stage, sort of a meditation." She raised her left leg and angled it across her body and bent her right knee. She stretched out her arms to her sides and turned her palms up. Blevins thought she looked like a dancing Shiva, but with tits and fewer arms. "Here's everyone's favorite," she said.

"'To be, or not to be: that is the question:
Whether 'tis nobler in the mind to suffer
The slings and arrows of outrageous fortune,
Or to take arms against a sea of troubles,
And by opposing end them? To die, to sleep;
No more; and by a sleep to say we end

The heart-ache, and the thousand natural shocks . . .' What's so funny?"

"I'm sorry," Blevins said. "I'm not laughing at you. You just have no idea how relevant that is to me right now."

Ophelia sat on the couch beside Blevins and took his hand. "I'm the one who should be sorry. Not exactly encouraging words for someone suffering from depression. Things especially rough right now?"

"It's a case I'm working on. Homicide."

"Someone you knew got murdered?"

Blevins stared at the wall and wondered if any men actually fantasized about Asian women with faces painted white and hair in buns. "No. I think I know someone involved."

"One of your cop friends."

"Worse. My daughter."

"The runaway?"

"Yes."

"Jesus, Harry, I mean, Blevins." Ophelia pulled his head onto her shoulder as if comforting a child. "Well, at least that means she's back. What are you going to do? You're not going to arrest her, are you?"

"I have no idea. I'm not even sure if I can find her."

"C'mon, now. You mean you're not like those—who is it, the Mounties?—always get their man, or girl? You could cover the whole thing up. Don't tell me you cops don't do that all the time." She ran her long, purple fingernails across his head. "This probably isn't doing your suicidal tendencies any good. Or, have you gotten over that?"

Blevins squeezed her hand. Despite all these visits, she had never touched him with such tenderness. "I think I'm better. My shrink thinks I've defined myself by my one great, well, I should say my greatest, blunder, instead of thinking of life as a series of redefinitions."

"I'm not sure I agree, dear. I think we all spend too much of our lives in denial and self-deception. I'd be lying to myself if I thought that I'm not really a stripper, that I'm *really* a teacher. Maybe what you're struggling with is the refusal to accept what you are, a wife killer."

Blevins sat up and looked her in the eyes. "My shrink would sure object to that approach. He'd probably remind me of what Jean-Paul Sartre said about bad faith, hiding behind roles."

"What are we other than the roles we create for ourselves? That's not bad faith. That's just basic human existence. How long have you been seeing this quack? How much money have you spent on him? I'm sure your *sessions* with me are a lot cheaper and a hell of a lot more fun. Tell me, who's been better for you?"

"You make a good argument."

"You mean I *give* good argument," she said and chuckled. "Know what else I 'm good at giving?"

Ophelia slid from the couch and onto the floor to keel between Blevins's legs. She unzipped his pants as Coltrane blew "Resolution."

FEBRUARY 2016

Gad came out of the shower with a towel around his waist and another wrapped around his dreadlocks. His beard, dyed in yellow and green stripes, dripped water onto the dragon tattoo on his chest. Diana wished she had had time to wash and dry his clothes before her mother returned home. She could at least give him a couple of her father's shirts.

"Where's my bag?" Gad asked.

"Under your clothes on the chair," Diana said.

Gad crossed the bedroom, tossed the clothes to the floor, and reached into a tan shoulder bag.

"That's a cool bag," Diana said.

"Made it myself," Gad said. "Hemp. I was going to color it, mabes like the seasons. Yellow for summer, brown for fall, white for winter, green for spring, but I kind of like the natch look. I could make you one."

"That'd be nice."

"Stone Sleeper usually has plenty of hemp. Makes sandals. She'll probs float me some." He sat beside Diana on the bed and opened a pack of cigarette papers. "You do it like this. Put the ends around your index fings like this and make a little trough. Be careful cause it'll tear easy. Pour some weed in here. Leave some room at the ends. Then roll it up. Careful, not too much presh. Lick the edge and stick it. Want to try?"

"Sure." Diana took the paper, filled it with weed from the plastic sandwich bag, rolled, licked, and sealed.

Gad laughed. "I think you've had some practice."

"A time or two."

Gad snapped open a matte black Star cigarette lighter.

"Wait," Diana said. "I think I heard the dog."

"Ha. All paras and not even had a toke."

"Don't light it yet," Diana whispered. "I'll take a look."

She left the bedroom and walked down the hall. She crept down part of the stairs, crouched to peer into the den, and saw Blevins plop onto the couch. She hurried, as quietly as she could, to her bedroom.

"Fuck. It's my father."

"The leo? I thought you said he was gone."

"Well he's back, goddamnit. You got to go."

Gad dropped the towels and put on his clothes. "How'm I gonna sneak by him?"

"You have to climb out the window." Diana pushed him across the room and opened the window. "It's not far down. Now come on."

Gad looked at the ground. "There's nothing to climb on."

"Then you just got to jump."

"Fucking Mother Moon."

He eased himself out, hung from the sill for a moment, then let go.

Diana was surprised by the loud thud. She thought she heard Gad emit a squeak upon impact. He lay on his back, trying to retrieve the wind that had been knocked out of him.

She dropped the bag onto Gad and pointed towards the neighbor's yard. She heard movement downstairs. Was it Apollo, or had her father heard the noise and was going to investigate? She watched Gad get to his feet and scamper across the back yard. He struggled to negotiate the chain link fence, fell into the neighbor's yard, and disappeared behind a boat shed.

Diana left her bedroom. Perhaps she could go downstairs and distract her father. She could tell him that she was awakened by a noise and saw a dog run across the back yard, probably the same one he had chased off a few days earlier. But what if he asked if her mother was asleep upstairs? She would have to say yes, and when he went to bed to find that his wife was not there, he would probably not suspect Diana of knowing anything.

As she got to the top of the stairs, she heard the television come on. If he had looked into the back yard, he must not have seen Gad, or he would have chased the Starlight, firing his gun into the darkness. She went back to her room to find the joint lying on the bed. Her father would hear the toilet if she flushed it, so she hid it under her pillow to be flushed in the morning.

She could not sleep. Why was her father home already? Was he waiting up to confront her mother when she returned home from her night with that man? Even if her father was too blind to notice what was happening under his nose, hell was going to break loose when her mother walked in.

Later as she was beginning to doze off, she was startled by *pop pop*. Was it a noise, or was it just that odd occurrence when you are nearly asleep and you awake suddenly as if you had been slapped? She heard voices. What if Gad had stupidly tried to sneak back in and her father had caught him? She got out of bed and went downstairs.

She found her father in the kitchen doorway, speaking into the telephone in his left hand. His right arm was extended as if pointing out something for her to see. She walked around her father, who did not seem to notice her, and saw her mother bunched on the kitchen floor, Apollo nudging her mother, and the mayor of Ocala leaning against the refrigerator, his hands above his head, his eyes and mouth a triangle of Os.

She looked back at her father and saw the pistol in his hand. She screamed.

"Get upstairs, Diana," Blevins said, as calmly as if he were simply telling her it was bedtime.

Diana stepped over her mother to take a butane lighter from the kitchen junk drawer. She lifted Apollo and went into the den and twirled a few times and hummed with the dog in her arms. Apollo was a bit excited, but his heartbeat was slowing down. She went upstairs and lit the joint.

★ ★ ★ ★ ★ ★ ★ ★ ★ ★ ★ ★ ★ ★ ★

"What time did your father return home?" the prosecutor asked.

"Around midnight I think," Diana said.

"Did you go downstairs to greet him?"

"No, sir. I was trying to get to sleep."

"How did you know it was him when you heard someone enter the house?"

"I went to the top of the stairs and saw him, but I just went back to bed."

"When your father took other trips, did he ever return home early or did he stay away as long as he said he would?"

Diana looked at Blevins, who was looking at a legal pad in front of him. "I don't know. I guess not."

"Did you know where your mother was at the time?"

"Yes, sir."

"And where was she?"

"She was with that man." Diana pointed to a man who sat behind the prosecutor's table.

"Let the record indicate that Miss Bombardi pointed out Mayor Farris Todd," Charlie Haskell said. "How did you know where your mother was?"

"I saw her get into his car in front of our house. He opened the door for her."

"Miss Bombardi, were you aware that your mother was having an affair with Mayor Todd?"

Diana looked at the jury. She recognized a woman who was a cashier at Walmart and a man who was a clerk at one of the clothing stores in the mall. An elderly woman cupped her ear as if, Diana thought, this might be the most important moment of the trial. "Yes."

"How did you know? Did your mother tell you?"

"She didn't tell me. I just figured it out. She worked late a lot, and never talked to Dad much. She would walk upstairs to bed and not even tell him goodnight. Sometimes when I was upstairs in bed and Dad was still downstairs, I could hear my mother in her room on the phone."

"Could she have been just talking to a friend?"

"My Dad and I used to laugh at Mom because she would talk real loud into the phone, like people in those old movies did. But these times that I'm talking about, she spoke low, almost like whispering. And she giggled. I'd never heard her giggle that way."

"Did your father know about your mother's affair?"

"He must have, because—"

"Objection!" Blevins's attorney said. "Speculation, Your Honor."

"Sustained," Judge Martin said.

"Miss Bombardi, did your father ever say to you that he suspected his wife was having an affair?"

"No, sir."

Haskell walked away from Diana and leaned against the rail in front of the jury. "Miss Bombardi, please tell the court what you heard and saw the night you lost your dear mother."

"Your Honor," Blevins's attorney said.

"Mr. Haskell," the judge said.

"Pardon me," Haskell said. "I mean, the night of your mother's death."

"I think I had just fallen asleep when a noise woke me up. Popping sounds. Then I heard voices downstairs, so I went to see what was going on. My father was standing in the doorway between the den and the kitchen. He was talking on the phone I guess to the sheriff's office."

"Miss Bombardi," Haskell said, "you can't be sure who he was talking to can you? For all you know it could have been a friend or maybe no one at all, right?"

"Your Honor, please!" Blevins's attorney said. "The court has established that Major Bombardi called the Sheriff's Department immediately following the shooting."

"Mr. Haskell," Judge Martin said, "let the young lady continue in her own words."

"Yes, Your Honor," Haskell said. He removed a handkerchief from his pocket. "Please continue, Miss Bombardi, and you look like you could use this." He approached the witness box and handed Diana the handkerchief.

"Oh, for Christ's sake," Blevins's attorney said.

"Mr. Simpson," Judge Martin said.

"I'm sorry, Your Honor," the attorney said.

Diana looked at the judge, who smiled and nodded at her. "I went to the kitchen, and I saw my mother on the floor and that man, Mayor Todd, standing behind her with his arms up in the air. My father told me to go back upstairs, so I did."

Haskell crossed the courtroom pinching his chin and looking down at the floor. "How did your father behave when you saw him in the kitchen? Did he appear to you to be upset? Angry?"

"He was calm, no expression, just like he is right now."

FEBRUARY 2018

The Pickin' Shack was once a garage in which Fatty Rowling used to park his tractor and four-wheelers before he shot out his own knee on a duck hunt, went on disability, and retired. Now with the vehicles and tools removed, the Shack sported neon beer signs, a menagerie of stuffed wildlife, and a concrete-top bar adorned with a poster from a failed restaurant that read "Yes We Have Cold Duck." Every Saturday night from Labor Day through Easter for the past five years, a dozen or more amateur musicians and forty or fifty others converged on Fatty's to play or listen to bluegrass music and enjoy the pot-luck dishes lining folding tables and the ribs and homemade sausage Drexel Henry served up from the massive smoker he towed behind his dualie. In previous Februarys, the participants sat inside the Shack to warm by electric space heaters. On this night, they gathered outside to jockey for spots near the three oscillating fans.

Blevins and Moreno arrived in Blevins's truck at eight PM. "The music should be starting about now," Blevins said. "Looks like a good sized crowd despite the heat. Grab that potato salad and a chair from the back."

Blevins pulled his guitar case from the back seat and a chair from the truck bed. They made their way through people seated in clumps and fanning themselves with caps and the church bulletins Fatty always passed around. Blevins shook hands, introduced Moreno, and then led the deputy into the Shack where he laid his guitar beside several others on an old telephone cable spool turned in its side to serve as a table. He placed his plastic container of store-bought potato salad by the bowls of homemade. He and Moreno ladled food onto their plates and threw a few dollars into the bucket to help Fatty with the incidentals like paper plates, plastic utensils, and general upkeep.

"Don't fill up until you get some ribs from Drexel at the smoker over there," Blevins told Moreno. "And don't forget the cooler of beer in the back of the truck if you want one."

They unfolded their chairs outside by an old hog trough now used as a foot rest by Hoyt and Yellow Kemp and as a spittoon by Edna Yancey. Moreno surveyed the crowd. The four old men from Krazy Karla's Kitchen sat by an old gasoline pump. They were talking loudly all at once, and Moreno suspected they were well into a few cups of something other than coffee. Several other groups of four or five people were scattered around the open area in front of the building, but most of the attendees arranged their lawn chairs in rows, theater-style, facing the open double doors.

A slap on the back caused Blevins to spill iced tea on his shirt.

"How's it hanging, sonny boy?" Fatty said. "Godamighty! Y'all about to catch that mystery woods killer? I hear you out there working it your own damn self."

Blevins turned to the smiling Fatty, whose metal hook where his left hand used to be was clamped onto a can of Pabst Blue Ribbon. "Mister Horace Rowling, I'd like you to meet Deputy Roberta Moreno who just joined the department. Mister Rowling owns this sad looking place."

"Everybody calls me Fatty, young lady," Fatty said, "but you can call me Mister Rowling." He rolled back his head with a laugh that stretched into a creaking sound much like a duck call. "I'm just shitting you, girlie. Godamighty! I hope you're not trying to learn anything from that old fool there, are you?"

"Well, I, uh . . ." Moreno said.

"Hey," Fatty said, "you enjoy yourself, hear? Anybody starts anything with you, 'cause of whatever, you let me know, and I'll run them off this place something fierce. Now how about that dead skunk ape fellow?"

"Yeah, Blevins," Yellow said. Her T-Shirt read "Old Gals Rule." "I hear that skunk ape about tore his head off."

Edna leaned over and spat into the trough and wiped her mouth on the shoulder of her lime green sun dress. "Listen, that skunk ape been killing up bears, too. That's what happens when you start messing with things you ought to be leaving alone. A durn shame."

Blevins swallowed and laid his plate onto his lap. "Now hold on. We're going to get whoever did it, but it wasn't a skunk ape that killed the man or the bears. Besides, we don't have any evidence right now to link the two things, unless the Game Commission has come up something and hasn't told us yet. Problem is, we can't get people out here to crack their mouths. We know that Boykin, the dead guy, talked to people, and if they'd just open up, we might get a clue."

"I seen him fussing with Mingo and that Hampton fellow when I was coming out of Winn Dixie," Edna said. "I was needing me some eggs. I can't hardly get going in the morning but I ain't got me an egg and a piece of toast for breakfast. They got that Roman Meal bread at the Winn Dixie. Best toast I ever eat. I done thought they stopped making it. But, listen, you know I ain't scared to talk about nothing. Sappy Goings, she was coming out of Winn Dixie, too, tried to hide the bottle of wine in her grocery bag but I seen it. I sure did. Anyhow, she told me who he was. Said he talked to her because somebody told him that she seen the skunk ape one time. Said he was trying to catch it. Sappy told him that old devil monster would eat him up before he even knew what had a hold of him."

"What did you hear them saying in the parking lot, Edna?" Blevins asked.

"Listen, I didn't hardly hear nothing. Didn't really give a durn neither. None of my business, you know what I'm saying? More people ought to keep to they own business. That's what that skunk ape man ought to done. Look what it got him." She looked at the Kemps. "Did that skunk ape man come to y'all's house? I remember hearing you say one time, Hoyt, you seen that old monkey thing walking the road."

"Is that who you was talking to out by the mailbox last week?" Yellow asked Hoyt. "Had on one those big old hats they wear when they hunt elephants."

"No," Hoyt said and stood. "Never met him. Hey, I got to go see a man about a dog." He left and walked to the back of the Shack.

"I reckon nature called him on a quick sudden, eh?" Fatty said and laughed. "Know what I think, Blevins? I believe it was one of them dadgum hippies. Godamighty, they all drugged up on Lord knows what. I see them thumbing in and out of town in they raggy ass clothes. I made the dadgum mistake of giving a couple of them a ride years ago. A girl and a boy, or I least I believe it was a boy. You can't hardly tell with them all got the same matted up hair, only most of the boys is got beards, at least a little more beard than the girls!" Fatty laughed and poked his hook into Moreno's side. "Liked to never got the smell out of my truck. Thought I was going to have to rip out the seats and burn them. It's got to where you can't hardly do a good deed for somebody without it coming back to bite you in your ripe old ass. You ought to haul them all in, Blevins. Somebody's gonna get tired of laying up in the jail cell and then they'll tell you who kilt that skunk ape chaser. Godamighty, ain't that right, Randy?"

"I'm not really sure," Moreno said. "And it's Roberta."

"It's fixing to get real randy in here once we get some music going! Whoo! Y'all hear what I said?" Fatty guffawed and turned towards several people standing by the Shack door. "Godamighty, Clint, what y'all waiting for?"

"We'd better play a few, everybody," a man sitting by the door said, "before Fatty gets all up in hisself and runs us off."

Blevins went into the Shack where others were removing their instruments from cases. Soon a small group gathered into a semi-circle in front of the Shack—five guitarists, two fiddlers, two banjo players, and one tiny woman on a tall stool with a double bass. They tuned for a moment, discussed their options for song selection, and kicked into "Lonesome Road Blues." A fiddler played a verse, then a banjo player, then one man began to sing: "I'm going down this road feeling bad
. . . ." After he sang two verses, claiming that he "ain't gonna be treated this a way," he nodded at Blevins, who took a step toward the audience and played the melody through a verse. The singer nodded at Blevins again, and this time Blevins picked a little more aggressively, throwing in a couple of blue notes and ending with a variation on a G run he had practiced that

afternoon. The other musicians smiled and nodded approval as the singer protested his being fed cornbread and peas.

"Pretty good, ain't he, Robin?" Yellow said to Moreno.

"Yes," Moreno said. "It's Roberta."

"You play anything?"

"I had a few guitar lessons a long time ago."

"You ought to get on up there then. We ain't had any, ah, young people playing in a long time."

"May I ask you something? How'd you get the name 'Yellow'?"

She sipped from a large insulated cup with "Hot Stuff" written in flames on it. "They been calling me that since I been a child. I'm too old to remember why."

"It's 'cause of them Chinaman eyes she got," Edna said. "We used to think she was retarded."

"Hush, Edna. You know I weren't never no retard."

The group played more bluegrass songs and a few country tunes. A banjo player sang George Jones's "Window Up Above," and the woman on bass did the Bill Anderson-penned, up-tempo "Slipping Away," which had the crowd clapping and stomping in rhythm. Moreno went to the smoker for a plate of ribs.

"Try one of these here sausage, too, sweetie," Drexel said. "Just don't ask what's in it. Blevins might have to run me in. Hoo yeah!" He winked at Moreno.

Moreno noticed someone in the shadows dart behind a pine tree about ten yards away. Probably just some drunk taking a pee, she thought.

She returned to her seat as Blevins announced that he would do a song everyone knew. He sang "Hold Back the Waters" by Florida's folk song hero Will McLean, and everyone around Moreno joined in on the chorus about the threat of a flood from the cold waters of Lake Okeechobee. When the song finished a woman yelled, "Sing us a gospel one, Blevins!"

Blevins fanned himself with his Tampa Bay Buccaneers cap. "I might need a little inspiration first," he said. He drew a leather-sheathed flask from his back pocket and had a swig. Giggles arose in the crowd. Blevins spoke to the other musicians and nodded to a fiddler who played a short intro. Blevins sang in a smooth baritone. "Some bright morning when this life is o'er," and everyone in the audience answered with "I'll fly away." Moreno felt oddly embarrassed, as if she were eavesdropping on a private and revealing conversation. When everyone else belted out the chorus, she pretended to know the lyrics and managed to sing the "I'll fly away"s at the right times. The others sang so loudly, with many standing and clapping, that she was reminded of the enthusiasm she had witnessed in the Pentecostal church in Atlanta. "The Holy Ghost is amongst us!" she remembered the preacher saying as he pranced around the pulpit. "He's reaching for your hand right now, brothers and sisters. Come down to the altar. Don't leave him hanging!"

Moreno scanned the excited faces and wondered how much of their energy was from the gospel song and how much was due to alcohol. The trash can with "Recycle" written in red, spray-painted letters was already filled with beer cans, beer bottles, and a few pint bottles that had held cheap bourbon. Beyond Drexel's smoker she saw a figure, shuffling, maybe dancing, by the trees. She wondered if it was the same person she had noticed there earlier. A vehicle pulled into the driveway, and its headlights swept across trees to illuminate the man among them—Purvis Driggers.

The musicians announced a short break, and Blevins returned to where Moreno sat.

"Having fun?" Blevins asked Moreno.

"I am, actually, but I need a word with you."

"You sounding real good, Blevins," Edna said. "I want you to do that one about the guy who goes out and shoots the girl with a .44 then tries to run away. What's it called?"

"That's 'Little Sadie,'" Yellow said. "I love that one too. They sure is a lot of songs about killing, ain't they? Mostly men killing women. Is they any about women killing men? I don't like to see no violence when I'm watching me a movie, but I sure do like me a murder song. What you think that says about me, Robin? Think I'm a crazy old woman? He he!"

"I wouldn't know," Moreno said. She stood and leaned towards Blevins. "Can we step over to your truck, Sir?"

They left the others and walked along the angled line of cars. Blevins lowered the tail gate of his truck and sat.

"This cracker music giving you the fidgets, Moreno?" Blevins asked. "We can go if it's stuck in your craw."

"My craw, Sir?" Moreno wondered if the Major always slipped into country jargon when he played music with the Forest people.

"Just an expression."

"I know. Listen, the Driggers man. He's here."

Blevins took a swallow from his flask and offered it to Moreno who shook her head. "Where is he?"

"I saw him by those trees over there behind the barbeque grill."

Blevins pocketed his flask and slipped off the tail gate. "Wait here. I'll go have a look."

Blevins walked in the narrow strip of weeds between the fronts of the cars and the ditch. When he was beyond the trees he circled back along the edge of the field and entered the clump of pines. He spotted Purvis a few yards ahead leaning with his ear against a pine as if listening for something in the trunk. Blevins moved as quietly as he could until he was a foot behind Purvis. He placed his hand on Purvis's shoulder. "Driggers."

"Hunk," Purvis grunted and slumped to his knees. His twisted his face around to look over his shoulder at Blevins. "Uuh. Scared me. Uuh."

"What the hell are you doing here, Driggers? I thought I told you to get your ass back home."

"Ooh," Purvis said. He put his hand on the tree, stood, spread his feet a yard apart, and slowly stood as if his legs were unsteady. "That so scared me I done shitted in my pants. My pants I got to get more."

Blevins smelled shit. "I warned you about following me, goddamnit."

"I think I was seeing her."

"Who? Martha?"

"Like she was young."

"Let's go. You staying in another hotel?"

"Hotel not them. My truck I'm staying back down the road and I walked in the ditch."

"Come with me."

Blevins led Purvis to where Moreno waited on the truck tail

gate. "I'm taking him to the department. Which way is your truck, Driggers?"

Purvis pointed.

"Give me your keys," Blevins said.

Purvis took a key ring from his pocket. He held it up by the Isuzu key. One other key and a naked woman carved from wood dangled from the ring.

"You take these," Blevins said to Moreno. "Can you drive a stick?"

"I think so," Moreno said.

"Stick on the floor," Purvis said. "Clutch and not the brake and then go first second third four."

"Get in the truck while I fetch my guitar," Blevins said.

Blevins got his guitar, told Fatty and a few others that he was needed back at the department, and came back to find Driggers in the back seat and Moreno standing outside with the door open.

"Let's go," Blevins said.

"I don't know if I can, Sir. It's foul in there."

"I scared the shit out him, literally. Hang your head out the window."

As they left the Pickin' Shack, Moreno pointed to the end of the line of vehicles. Mingo Mauser leaned against the grill of his truck, his hand high in the air, his middle finger extended.

"Too bad we missed his visit," Blevins said.

Mingo lowered his arm and pointed at them as they drove by. Moreno could see someone sitting in Mingo's truck. She thought it was a woman, but she was not certain.

They found the Isuzu a quarter of a mile down the road. Moreno got out, and Blevins turned his truck around a waited for Moreno to get into Purvis's truck. Moreno cranked it, and the little Pup bucked onto the road with a squeal of the tires. It bucked each time Moreno changed gears but finally leveled out to a smooth sixty miles an hour through the hot Forest night.

"This a guitar I know like my brother he got," Purvis said. "Where we going?"

"I'm taking you to the Sheriff's Department so you don't have to sleep in your truck tonight. Tomorrow you'll be on your way back home. Understand?"

"They gotten pants for me and to be taking these off?"

"We'll get you cleaned up. Did you have any supper tonight?"

"I eat today nothing. She in that truck I seen her with the big man was shooting the bird."

"Who?"

"Martha but not her. Look like young Martha but not."

"Get that out of your head."

★ ★ ★ ★ ★ ★ ★ ★ ★ ★ ★ ★ ★ ★

"Get this fellow cleaned up and put him in a cell," Blevins said to Sergeant Dalton.

"Parson Brown," Dalton said. "He is one rank individual. Whew! If we're bringing them in for stinking, we're going to need a whole lot bigger facility."

"I'll be in to deal with him first thing in the morning. Get him something to eat, too."

Dalton buzzed open the door and took Purvis to the back.

"Give me his keys," Blevins said to Moreno. "Come on and I'll drop you off at home."

They climbed into Blevins's truck. "Still smells horrible in here," Moreno said. "You going back out to play some more, Sir?"

"Naw. Think I'll turn in early."

"OK, Reverend."

"What's that?"

"Sergeant Dalton called you Parson Brown. Is that your secret alias?"

"He wasn't calling me that," Blevins said. "Just an old expression for people who don't use 'Jesus Christ.' Like some people say 'John Brown.' Parson Brown is actually a breed of orange developed by a man in Florida named Parson Brown. He was—"

"Major, I know all that. I was just messing with you."

"Oh. Sorry. I was just going off on another lecture, or in this case, a sermon, eh?"

Moreno nodded. "You're learning."

Purvis stood in the center of the cell and considered his accommodations. A cot, a toilet, and a sink against a cement block wall with bars for walls on the other three sides. He liked Lieber Correctional better. It had four real walls like a room should have. Lieber had bunk beds where Dog Eye slept on the bottom and Purvis slept on top. Here, he could see men in the cells on either side of him here, and that somehow made him lonely. One man was asleep in just his underwear, and the other man sat on his cot reading a book.

"What you reading that book?" Purvis asked. "Name of Purvis Driggers and not here I don't live just looking for people."

The man neither answered nor looked up.

"You know that sheriff his name Bombardi he brung me in here." Still no reaction from the other man. "I shitted in these pants I was scared and they giving me more and some supper." Purvis stepped towards the bars separating him from the man.

The book sailed spine first through the bars and flipped and spread like wings just as it hit Purvis in the face. He fell onto his back with the open book covering his eyes. He lifted it a few inches off his face.

"This a Bible I readed it in Lieber Correctional. They hit me with other things there."

JANUARY 2018

Purvis recognized the faces at the long table. He knew the names of Warden Bunch and Dr. Gethers but not the others. He had been told their names before, but he remembered them by the impressions they made upon him: Mean Man, Staring Man, Lots of Questions Man, and Lady with the Papers. Dog Eye had said that the Board was going to decide if Purvis should be released. Purvis wondered which one was named The Board. If it was Mean Man, Purvis figured, he would be at Lieber Correctional for a long time to come.

"I'm having difficulty understanding how you can conclude that this man is sane, Doctor," Mean Man said. "He can't even speak intelligibly."

Purvis did not know what kind of speaking Mean Man was talking about. Purvis spoke from his mouth like everyone else.

"Admittedly," said Dr. Gethers, "his speech, especially his syntax, is idiosyncratic. On the other hand, he performs his tasks perfectly well. Frampton can verify this."

The warden tapped the screen of his laptop. "His performance at the prison farm is impeccable. He operates the tractors, manages the irrigation system, does all manner of repairs on the machinery. Hell, he practically runs the place. Follows orders and never any goldbricking."

Purvis wished he had a little folding computer like the warden's. He had learned a few things about using a computer. He could turn one on and find information fast, much faster than you can at a library. He could find books on the computer, except they were not the kinds of books with paper pages, and if you start to read one, it was hard to tell how much more you had to read before you finished it. Purvis had not finished any of those computer books, but you did not have to worry about losing the book. You could turn off the computer and then some other day, if you remembered the name of the book, it would still be in the computer. You could even watch little movies on those computers that looked sort of like televisions at the prison library. Purvis thought that the warden's little folding computer was so skinny that it could not have very many books and movies in it.

"So you would say that he could hold down a job?" Questions Man asked.

"Easily," said Warden Bunch. "I'd say he could be a successful handyman. He might need someone else to keep an eye on his finances, but no doubt he could find work for himself."

Purvis liked the word "handyman." He thought about the shirts that the propane truck drivers wore with their names written above the pocket. He used to drive those trucks but just part-time and so never got one of those fancy shirts. If he went back home and did handyman work, he would by God get him a shirt with "Handyman" over one pocket and "Purvis" over the other. He could have a pack of cigarettes in the pocket under "Handyman" and a pencil and tire gauge in the one under "Purvis." His name would have to be written high enough so that the pencil would not stick up and cover part of it. He would not want people to think his name was "urvis."

"But the fact that you doubt he could attend to his finances," Mean Man said, "seems to me to speak against his ability to prosper autonomously."

"Hell, Lou," the warden said, "I can't keep up my own finances!" Everyone laughed, so Purvis did, too.

"Perhaps Mr. Driggers would like to speak to this," said Staring Man. His gaze had not shifted from Purvis the entire meeting, which Purvis judged to have been either fifteen or fifty minutes.

"Driggers," the warden said, "would you like to tell the Board if you could take care of money if you are released?"

So, Staring Man must be The Board, Purvis thought. He was happy that Mean Man was not The Board. "Yes, Sir."

After a moment Warden Bunch said. "Well, go ahead then."

"See they got them banks for you take money and that go in there then give a check you write on it the how much and pay things."

"You are saying that you could pay your bills with checks, right?" Dr. Gethers asked.

"I am saying."

Mean Man leaned back in his chair and sighed. "See what I mean? That was pretty much gibberish. What do you think, Helen?"

Papers Lady removed her glasses and placed them on the top of her head. Purvis thought that made her look smart. If he ever had to have glasses, he would do the same when he talked to people. He would also have a clipboard like hers with a pen on a beaded chain attached to it.

"I think we should maintain a certain formality," she said. "This is a serious affair of the state. This gentleman's freedom is at stake. Now, his manner of speaking is indeed peculiar, but that's not a proper criterion for our decision today. The focus is his work performance and behavior during his incarceration, particularly recently. According to his files, he has been a model inmate. No disciplinary action in the entire ten years. If Dr. Gethers is confident in Mr. Driggers's mental state, then so am I. You are confident, aren't you, Dr. Gethers?"

Gethers took a deep breath. He looked at Purvis and made a soft clucking sound with his tongue. Purvis made the same clucking sound and smiled.

"I find no behavioral issues," Gethers said. "My one concern, which is not a very serious one, is his obsession with someone who may be from his past or could be only his imagination. Frankly, I can't tell. I suspect, however, that it is a coping mechanism. Inmates commonly construct a goal, almost a reason for being, if you will, that gives them some hope for the future. Sometimes it's about atonement. They may rehearse a speech they plan to give to their families or to victims of their crimes. Others have an elaborate plan for starting life anew, perhaps relocating to the Caribbean to build boats. These fantasies are almost always harmless and rarely, despite popular myth, involve revenge. Unfortunately, they are almost never realized upon release, but they serve their purpose to keep up the inmate's morale. I'm in danger of abusing doctor patient privilege here, but Mr. Driggers often speaks of a woman whom he believes is waiting for him. I said a moment ago that he was obsessed, but that might be putting it too strongly. I recommend that he continue some form of counseling upon his release, I mean, of course, if he is released, but I'm sure he will soon forget about it."

"But what if he doesn't?" Questions Man asked. "Any likelihood that he might track down this person and, who knows?"

"No history of violence," Warden Bunch said. "I think we've heard enough to have a vote. What do you think?" The others all nodded. "Driggers, would you please step out for a moment? The guard is waiting outside the door."

★ ★ ★ ★ ★ ★ ★ ★ ★ ★ ★ ★ ★ ★

"You gonna miss me, Purv?" Dog Eye asked. He lay on his side on the cot with his face nearly touching the wall as usual. Most of the time Purvis was unsure if Dog Eye was sleeping or awake, but Purvis knew that Dog Eye did not like to be disturbed from his naps, so Purvis was careful to be quiet when in the cell.

"Everybody, yeah."

"That's funny, Purv. Your mama coming to get you?"

"You know dead is my Mama. I call DeWayne my brother with his new car for tomorrow and take me home."

"Don't be surprised if he don't show up. He's been shed of you for ten years. Might be got used to not seeing your ugly ass face around."

Purvis eased onto his cot, as if he still thought Dog Eye might be asleep. "DeWayne be here. My brother. Then he give me that truck and I can drive."

"Then you gonna take that truck to find that girl, eh? I hear she's been making a good living sucking dick. But she ain't got nothing on you in that department. Maybe you can steal her customers. You tell the Board what a champion cocksucker you are? That's your good behavior."

Purvis knew that Dog Eye was lying about Martha. Dog Eye almost never got to leave the cell, and he had not had a visitor in years. How could he have heard anything about her?

Purvis remembered the time he saw Sugar Boy kill Pinion with a spoon. Sugar Boy leaned across the table and stuck out his arm like he was swatting a mosquito from Pinion's neck. Sugar Boy sat back down and scooped some mashed potatoes with the same spoon. Blood poured from Pinion's throat all over his Thanksgiving turkey. It looked like he had smeared cranberry sauce on the slices of meat. Pinion stared down at his plate, and Purvis wondered if Pinion was more upset about his spoiled food than about the hole in his neck. Purvis took his napkin from his lap and pressed it to the puncture in Pinion's neck, but the blood kept pumping out. A guard cracked Sugar Boy on the head with a metal baton and Sugar Boy fell against the table, knocking milk onto Purvis's lap. The napkin would have caught the milk if Purvis had not moved it to Pinion's throat. Two guards grabbed Pinion and dragged him away, maybe to the hospital but probably too late, Purvis thought. Purvis finished his Thanksgiving meal except for the cranberry sauce.

A spoon. Could Purvis shove a spoon into Dog Eye's neck? He had thought about this many times since Sugar Boy stuck Pinion. Now he was about to be released, so maybe the warden would not care much if Purvis killed Dog Eye. Purvis would not do it in the cafeteria, though. Sneaking a spoon back to the cell would be easy. He could stick Dog Eye at night while he slept, and maybe nobody would even know until after DeWayne had come to get Purvis and they were long gone. But which end of the spoon should he use, the eating end or the holding end? Sugar Boy was still in solitary, so Purvis could not ask him how to use it.

Dog Eye stood up, pulled down his pants, and then sat on the edge of his cot. "Come on, Purv. Time for you to give me a goodbye present."

Purvis wished he had a spoon.

"What the hell was the problem?" DeWayne asked. "I was here at ten o'clock just like you said and then I had to sit in that damn room there and look at all them bastards chained to benches. Here it is four o'clock and I ain't had nothing to eat but a honey bun from the gas station this morning."

DeWayne's car felt good to Purvis. The prison bus that he rode to the farm had hard seats with holes in them. The bus bounced with any little bump in the road, but the driver told Purvis to shut up when Purvis had suggested that the shocks needed to be replaced. The seats in DeWayne's car looked like leather, but Purvis thought they might be some kind of special plastic made just for car seats. The ride was so smooth and quiet that you might fall asleep as you drove.

"Spoon in my pants after breakfast I was taking back. They got mad. Said might have to keep me."

"Spoon?"

"Stick it in Dog Eye his neck. But that guard see me what we call Bone Breaker and had to talk with the warden and them. Then the warden he say to go."

"How much more eat up with the dumbass can you get? They were fixing to turn you loose and you were going to try and kill a guy. With a spoon? Dripping Jesus."

"You don't know it. Don't know nothing you don't." Purvis thought about Jesus dripping blood. He knew that Jesus had been nailed up high on a pole, and he remembered something a Sunday School teacher had said about somebody stabbing Jesus too. That was way back millions of years ago and they probably did not even have spoons then.

DeWayne lit a cigarette. "I know enough not to ruin my chances of getting released by doing something that damn stupid." He handed the pack of cigarettes and lighter to Purvis. "Reach back there in that cooler and grab us a couple of beers."

Purvis wondered why the car did not have a cigarette lighter in the dashboard. Maybe DeWayne had saved money and bought the cheaper model. There was no tape player in it either. DeWayne's Isuzu Pup had a tape deck, and it was over twenty years old. He lit a cigarette and got two bottles of beer from the cooler in the back seat. Michelob Ultra. Purvis remembered that Michelob was a special beer that he and DeWayne would drink if DeWayne made some overtime. "Ultra" must mean that it was extra expensive. Purvis smiled—DeWayne had done something nice for Purvis on his first day of freedom.

"So what you gonna do now?" DeWayne asked.

Purvis swallowed half the bottle of beer in one gulp. "Martha going to find her."

"Fuck me running! I ought to slap that shit right out of your head. That bullshit with her was—what?—twenty years ago? You never even spoke her goddamnit name after all that until a couple of years ago. The last few times I came to visit you all you did was babble about Martha. 'Martha loves me. Martha's waiting for me.' Martha's married and what's more is that she and her husband have been gone a long time. I think they went to Mexico or somewhere. So she's gone. Get used to it. You hear me?"

Purvis finished the beer and lowered his window with the button on the arm rest. He pushed the button again to raise the window, then pushed it again to lower it and threw the bottle out. It hit the "Jedburg Road" sign. He got another beer. "Florida."

"Jesus buttfucking Mother Mary! Can't you keep anything straight? Martha and her husband came back from Florida way before you went to prison. And another thing, for that matter, you're still married."

"Marie she left when I get doing time. Say she can't love her no convict."

"I know that," DeWayne said. "I'm going to stop at a Hardee's or whatever we pass next. I got to get a mouthful of something. Marie might change her mind now that you're out. I think she's living just over in McClellanville."

"On Marie I'm not giving a shit. Don't think about her I never even one time. She can be for a living sucking dick and I'm never giving one shit."

"Ha! Well, sounds like you're damn well over her, so you can just do the same with Martha. But if I were you, I'd go see Marie. She might give you some nookie for old time's sake.

That'll take your bent up mind off of that long gone bitch Martha. There's us a Burger King right yonder. I bet you never got a good hamburger at Lieber."

"I want Co-cola," Purvis said. He wondered if Martha drank Co-colas down in Florida. Florida was a place where people lived at the beach and ate giant oranges and coconuts and never had to work. He would pour her a Co-cola into one of those skinny glasses like rich people drank champagne out of when the ladies wore black dresses with feathery collars and long white gloves that went up to their elbows and the men wore those fancy black suits with bow ties. But he and Martha would not dress like that. She would wear a long yellow dress with purple dolphins on it, and he would wear short pants every day, not cut off dungarees but the real kind of short pants, plaid, that do not need a belt to stay up. He would grab a swordfish out of the water and carve it up like steaks and cook it on a grill for her, and she would say, "Oh my Purvis, you found me and you are so much my only man."

"Are you getting out of the fucking car or what?" DeWayne said.

Purvis opened his door. "A fish sandwich for me I'm eating."

FEBRUARY 2018

"I guess you saw the guys from FDLE going through everything," Sheriff Todd said. "Any chance we're going to put this thing to bed soon?"

"Unlikely," Blevins said. He knew that the Sheriff feared that the Florida Department of Law Enforcement might find something his Major Crimes Division had overlooked and solve the case. Blevins would have to hear Todd's angry lecture about the Department being embarrassed.

"You've interviewed them Starlights?"

"Got most of my Evidence Team doing that, if you can call them inter-views. You know how they are, can't get anything out of those kids."

"How about the locals?"

"Same. Our victim had limited contact with them, and they're all pretty tight-lipped, too."

Todd marked through something on his desk calendar. "They aren't too tight-lipped about calling here asking why we don't go out there and kill the skunk ape before it kills again. It's bad enough without having to deal with all that superstitious shit. Hear me? This thing's turning into a bad dream. The paper's doing a big old story on it, calling it the Skunk Ape Murder Mystery, throwing it together with them dead bears and monkeys like it was all part of the same thing. Up to sixteen bears now and twenty-nine monkeys. They had them woods full of game wardens and a dozen of our men I pulled off the road the last two nights with infrared binoculars and ain't not a single damn body seen a thing until they found more dead bears come morning light. I need you to close this case one way or another before they make us look like a bunch of hick fools."

"We'll wrap it up somehow."

"Get me a suspect. I don't care who or how. Just bring some son of a bitch in so it looks like we know what the hell we're doing. I got enough to worry about with this hurricane and that goddamn preacher setting up at Silver Springs. Hear me? We already got tour busses hauling in holy rollers all the way from Alabama and Tennessee. That mess we had when Willie Nelson was here last year with them five thousand pot heads is going to be nothing compared to this."

★ ★ ★ ★ ★ ★ ★ ★ ★ ★ ★ ★ ★ ★ ★

Purvis squatted like a baseball catcher in the middle of his cell.

"You ready to go home now, Driggers?" Blevins asked through the bars.

"Home. South Carolina my home. Florida not."

Blevins unlocked the door and stepped inside the cell. "A hurricane's on the way. You need to get on out ahead of it."

"Rain wall."

"Something like that. Now get out of those jail clothes. I brought you a shirt and some pants. They'll be big on you, but they'll do."

Purvis slipped the gray shirt over his head. "Like a doctor."

"Yes. They look like hospital scrubs, but I brought you some regular clothes. Now come on and let's get your wallet and stuff and get you on your way."

"My way."

Outside Blevins handed Purvis his keys and three twenty dollar bills. "That ought to get you enough gas to get back home. I want you to promise me that you're leaving Florida and going straight home today. OK?"

"OK."

"You promise?"

"Promise."

"That road out there will take you to I-75. Take that to I-10 to Jacksonville to I-95. Got it?"

"It." Purvis got into the Isuzu and left the parking lot.

Blevins watched him turn onto the road in the direction of the interstate.

"Think that's the last of him, Major?" Moreno asked.

Blevins had not noticed Moreno and wondered if the deputy had seen him give Purvis the money. "I believe so. That night in the jail cell probably convinced him that we're serious. I didn't think you were on duty today. Shouldn't you be in church?"

"Lieutenant Jacobs called and said FDLE was here. Said she needed help keeping an eye on them."

"Everybody gets nervous when they drop in. We usually get a little notice, but I think this time they didn't call until late yesterday. They'll go over everything and ask us a passel of dumb questions."

"Are they going to take the case from us?"

"I hope so, but I doubt it. Not much for them to work with. Let's go see if we can be of service."

★ ★ ★ ★ ★ ★ ★ ★ ★ ★ ★ ★ ★ ★ ★

Blevins did not recognize the number on his ringing cell phone. He answered.

"It's Wind Walker. You asked me to call if the dog dancer came back."

"She there now?"

"I guess they're still there, but I had to walk a long way to get phone service."

"They?"

"Her and that big regular, you know the one that chased Ricky? They're passing out flyers about some religious rally in town. He said he'll pile up as many in the back of his truck as want to go."

"Did they arrive at the camp together?"

"Yeah. Then the dog dancer—she won't say what her name is—picked up Jard's dog Frank, it's one of those wiener dogs, and danced with it and said that Frank was worried that God was about to pour his wrath upon us unless we repent and that Frank wanted some real meat to eat instead of the dry stuff Jard feeds him. I've never seen anything like it. That dog tries to bite anybody who gets near him, but he just let her pick him up like she'd raised him from a puppy."

"I'm on my way," Blevins said. "And thank you."

"Listen." Wind Walker paused. "Remember how you said you could help me get out of Babylon, I mean, back home? Did you mean that?"

"Of course."

"I'm ready."

★ ★ ★ ★ ★ ★ ★ ★ ★ ★ ★ ★ ★ ★

The digital light on the rearview mirror read 96 for an outside temperature when Blevins arrived at the Starlight camp. The skies were overcast, though, which might provide some slight relief, Blevins thought. As he got out of the car, he picked up a discarded flyer that announced Reverend Pyron's "Sermon at the Springs" in which the preacher, "The Lips of the Lord," will reveal why God has chosen to unleash the forces of nature upon a sinful people and what can be done to stem God's temper and "restore LIFE to a corrupt and dying nation." Also appearing would be Senator Robert Way and Corey Clayton, a former child actor who had who had left the sit com business to produce and star in Christian horror films based on the Book of Revelation and entitled The Truth series. Blevins was surprised that this trio had not dubbed itself The Way, The Truth, and The Life.

Mingo and the girl had already left. Blevins wandered through the camp, asking questions and getting no helpful answers. Several Starlights acknowledged having spoken to Mingo and the girl and having accepted their flyers, only to toss them into the fire moments later. Blevins showed pictures of Diana again, but all denied ever seeing her or seeing a resemblance between the pictures and the dog dancer.

Tock and two other young men approached Blevins.

"You sure do like us, don't you, brother Leo?" Tock said. One of Mingo's flyers was stuffed into the twine that cinched up the waist of what looked like an ancient Roman tunic. "I thought that you and your leo minions were finally done harassing us."

"Did you talk with Mingo, the regular who was just here, and the outlier girl?"

"Settle down, brother. You seem a little brusque today. Is it something at work?"

The two Starlights with Tock laughed. Blevins stepped forward to lean in, nearly touching Tock's face. Tock drew his head back and squinted as if a flashlight shown into his eyes.

"I've had enough of this uncooperative bunch!" Blevins said. He was three or four inches taller than Tock and at least forty pounds heavier, and he was sure the Starlight was feeling the intended intimidation. "You're going to talk to me or I'll take you in for obstruction of justice. Some of your associates here know that we can make things pretty uncomfortable for you there." Twenty or more Starlights had stopped what they were doing to stand a few yards away in witness. "Now, tell me, did the regular and the outlier girl come here together today?"

Tock's eyes darted towards his friends' faces, but none appeared to offer any sign of help. "Yes."

"Does she look like the girl in this picture?"

Tock wrinkled his brow. "Maybe. The dog dancer has long black hair. This picture has shorter hair and it looks lighter."

"Did she leave with the regular?"

"Yes. Left with him in his truck."

"OK." Blevins took a step away from Tock. The group around them was well over a hundred now. He did not see Wind Walker among them. He turned and walked towards the gate, Starlights moving aside to make a wide path for him.

"Wait!" Tock called. "You think that outlier killed the beast chaser, don't you? Is that what this is about? Why do you keep asking about the girl?"

Blevins got to his car. He took a pill from his pocket and the bottle from under the seat.

* * * * * * * * * * * * * *

A quarter mile from the Starlight camp someone emerged from the line of trees beside the road. Blevins watched the figure hop across the narrow ditch and stand in the strip of weeds between the tire ruts. He stopped the car a few yards in front of Wind Walker. She wore the same floppy hat but with jeans, T-shirt, and tennis shoes. A bulging tie-died bag was slung across her shoulder. Blevins waved her into the car, and she climbed in.

"You really were ready, weren't you?"

"Since I talked to you all I can think about is my daughter, Alanis, I haven't seen in three years. She's nine now. And this hurricane coming. I've never been in one before, but I know they come in the summertime not like now. What if those religious prophesies are right?"

"Put on your seatbelt."

"Oh yeah." She snapped the belt closed, turned to face the windshield, and placed her hands upon her knees. "I mean, it *could* happen, right?"

A deputy on the radio said that he was stopping a truck on State Road 40 just east of Mill Dam Lake for having no brake lights on its boat trailer.

"What could happen?" Blevins asked.

"The end of the world! I don't usually go for that organized religion stuff, but why take a chance? That regular with the dog dancer sure believes in it. I don't think I've ever met somebody so religious who could be so foul-mouthed. He called us some real ugly things. But what if he's right and the apocalypse happens and I never get to see Alanis again? I could be back home by tomorrow morning on the bus."

"I'll take you to the bus station later," Blevins said, "but I need to stop somewhere first."

They pulled off the dirt road and onto State Road 40 and saw turkey vultures gathered around a deer carcass on the sandy shoulder.

"Those birds as *so* ugly," Wind Walker said.

"I thought the Family members were supposed to love all forms of nature."

"I'm no longer in the Family. I'm back to my original name now. Ruth."

Just as they passed the feeding birds, a bald eagle swooped down. Some of the buzzards hopped aside to make room.

"A sign!" Ruth said.

Blevins laughed. "An eagle scavenging? Hardly a sign of anything except that it's hungry."

"But I thought eagles were, what's the word I want?, majestic birds of prey."

"Everything gets eaten by everything else out here."

The deputy was back on the radio saying that he had found a dead bear in the boat and had cuffed the two truck passengers. Blevins picked up the radio. "Pickens, it's Bombardi. Unhitch the boat trailer from the truck, get all these guys' info, and give them a good scare about possessing a bear and possible jail time and such. Then send them on their way. Maggie, notify the park rangers and the Game Commission and tell them Pickens is waiting with the boat for them."

"Send them on their way?" Deputy Pickens asked. "But, Major, what if these are the guys who've been killing all the bears?"

"They aren't. If they were, why'd they leave all the others in the woods and taken just this one? Maggie, send somebody out with a truck to haul the boat to the lot."

"Somebody's killing all the bears?" Ruth asked.

Blevins returned the radio handset to its hook. "Somebody's trying to."

"Why?"

"Don't really know. My hunch is that it's somebody's crazy notion of putting the wrath of God into people to manipulate them into . . . hell, I don't know."

"Wrath of God. Been hearing a lot about that lately."

Blevins accelerated the car to 90. "Seems to be the only thing that keeps some folks happy."

★ ★ ★ ★ ★   ★ ★ ★ ★ ★   ★ ★ ★ ★ ★

A dozen or more cars and trucks were parked in Mingo's yard. Blevins stopped behind a GMC pickup with oversized tires and a bumper sticker that read "I'm Ready To Meet Jesus! ARE YOU??" He lowered both the front windows and told Ruth to wait in the car.

As Blevins walked to the house he heard a voice from inside saying something about preparations and triumph. When he stepped onto the porch the voice stopped, and he heard a scraping noise like a chair across a wooden floor and the sound of a door slamming shut. Before he could knock, the front door opened.

"I doubt that you're here for our special prayer service," Mingo said. His powder blue shirt was stuck to his belly with sweat. The tail was untucked and the sleeves were rolled up past his elbows. Blevins thought he had never before seen Mingo wearing a shirt with a collar.

"Who was with you at the Starlight camp this morning?" Blevins saw people in the room behind Mingo craning their necks.

Mingo closed the door behind him. "None of your damn business. We're doing the Lord's work in here, but you wouldn't know nothing about that, would you? Now show me a warrant or get the hell off my property. Your day is coming soon enough."

The door opened and a man with a Bible in his hand stepped out. "Good afternoon, Sheriff. I'm Pastor Campbell. How can we help you?"

"Can't nobody or nothing help him," Mingo said.

Campbell smiled and put his hand on Mingo's shoulder. "You'll have to forgive Brother Mauser here. He's a little, well, high strung. Brother Mauser, we should invite the Sheriff in for some fellowship, don't you think?"

"I appreciate that, Pastor," Blevins said, "but I'm here on official business, looking for this girl." He held up his cell phone.

Campbell handed the Bible to Blevins. "Hold this for me, please." He slid down the glasses that were on the top of his head and took the phone from Blevins's hand. He held it close to his face, then at arm's length, and then up close again. "Let's see now." He looked up at Mingo. "Can't say for sure, but this might be Sister Goolsby's daughter. Karen I think her name is. She's right inside. Let me get her."

The preacher went into the house and returned in a moment with a blond girl in her late teens. "My mistake, it's Cathy, but now that I see her again, I don't think she's who you're looking for, Sheriff."

The girl's lips quivered as if she were about to cry.

"It's OK, young lady," Blevins said. "You can go back in." He mopped his sweaty face with a handkerchief.

"I'm sorry that we can't be of more assistance, Sheriff," Pastor Campbell said. "I'll take my Bible back now, but let me give you this." He handed Blevins a flyer. "You probably already know about our rally tomorrow. You've never seen anything like it around here and might never will again."

Blevins heard a car door close.

"Look! She's there!"

He turned to see Ruth running through the cars and pointing to the side of the house.

"The outlier!" Ruth shouted. "I saw her!"

Blevins jumped down from the porch and ran to the side of the house.

"Hey!" Mingo yelled.

Blevins saw no one in the side yard. He ran to the back and to the shed.

"Keep out of there!" Mingo shouted behind Blevins.

No one was in the shed. Several people came out of the back door of the house. Blevins ran from the shed and into the woods. "Stop!" he yelled. He was already panting. The thick undergrowth of palmettos and ferns amidst the pines and sweet gums seemed to hold in the humidity and turn the forest into a furnace.

"Diana!" he called. He knew Mingo would be behind him and wondered if the big man still had some of the speed he showed on the football field.

Nausea swept over Blevins, but he ran, looking for any glimpse of movement. She could have ducked behind a clump of palmettos and then circled back to the house. Even if he saw her, would he have any hope of chasing her down? If he fired a warning shot, would she take his bluff and halt?

He threw up before he could stop running. He was dizzy. His face was on fire. His gasps drew little air into his lungs. A pain streaked through his left arm just before he hit the ground.

★ ★ ★ ★ ★ ★ ★ ★ ★ ★ ★ ★ ★ ★ ★

Blevins heard low beeps as he opened his eyes and tried to focus. He was on his back and famished.

"Major?"

His head felt heavy as he turned to see Moreno standing over him. Moreno disappeared as Blevins realized that he was in a hospital room. In a few seconds a nurse was at his side.

"Just relax, Mr. Bombardi," the nurse said. She held his wrist. "You had a minor heart attack. No permanent damage best we can tell. Pulse a little high, but that's expected." She wrapped a sphygmomanometer around his arm. "162 over 118, but that should come down soon. Are you on blood pressure medication?"

"Yes."

"Our records say you suffered a similar episode two years ago. How about alcohol consumption? None, moderate, heavy?"

Blevins laughed. "Long time law enforcement. What do you think?"

The nurse did not laugh. "The doctor's going to tell you to quit and probably lose a few pounds. Smoker?"

"Cigar every now and then."

"Sheriff Todd's on his way," Moreno said from the foot of the bed.

"Are you allergic to any medication?" the nurse asked.

"No."

"Doctor Navarro will be here shortly," the nurse said and left.

Blevins raised his head and looked around the room. "Where's that girl?"

"The Starlight?" Moreno asked. "Somebody questioned her and brought her in here, but I think she's gone. She called the department on your radio after you fell out." She moved to the side of the bed and sat. "So, Sir, what was going on at that Mauser guy's house?"

Blevins saw the clock on the wall. 7:22. "Is it still Sunday?"

"Yes, Sir."

Blevins hoped that Ruth had made it to the bus station. He wondered if she had told anyone about seeing the "outlier" at Mingo's house. Did Diana know that he had collapsed while chasing her? Would she have worried that her father may have died trying to bring her back home? Did she have any idea, did she care, that he had spent two years searching the country for her?

The doctor came to the room and explained that the heart

attack had probably been triggered by heat exhaustion. He had seen quite a number of cases in the past two weeks, especially from middle aged men, of dehydration, heat stroke, and heart attacks. Blevins was lucky this time, the doctor said, but men of his age need to respect their physical limits. He wanted to monitor Blevins overnight, and chances were good that he would be discharged in the morning.

"I'd like to go now," Blevins said.

"Bad idea," Dr. Navarro said. "Sometimes another attack can follow soon. Aftershock if you will. I don't expect that, but let's play it safe. I recommend that you take a day or two off." He opened a folder and glanced down a page. "You check your blood pressure regularly?"

"Every few days or so."

"Do it twice a day, just after you wake up and again in the afternoon. Keep a log and show it to your personal care physician."

Blevins was given the same advice at his triennial visits to his doctor. Dr. Holmes, who had recently retired after nearly fifty years of practice, was old school—not recommending or advising, but insisting and lecturing. "You forget your daddy died in his forties from heart failure?" Dr. Holmes would say. "How you think this bodes for your hard-headed ass? He wouldn't listen to a goddamned thing I told him, and you're just like him in every way. Top of that, you're in a profession not known for longevity. You know, don't you, that most law men die within five years of retirement? That's if they make it to retirement. The ones what live to a ripe old age have to work hard at it, and that's not a goddamned bit what the hell you're doing. Look at you. Sedentary, hard drinker—I can't blame you too much on that one. Hell I throw back a couple myself when I get home after dealing with dumb assholes like you—and when's the last time you had a son-of-a-bitching salad?"

Dr. Holmes never mentioned that Blevins's father was also a wife killer who died in prison. Blevins had suffered no health problems before Sue's death. Had any life expectancy statistical research been done on men who kill their wives?

Dr. Navarro left. Blevins saw Senator Way on the television across the room. He found the remote attached to the bed rail and turned on the sound. The news anchor said that Way was the subject of ridicule for introducing a bill declaring that "'the beast known as the Sasquatch, the Big Foot, the Missing Link, and other names does not exist.' Way is best known for his eighteen-hour filibuster to overturn the Roe v. Wade decision and his ongoing attempts to dissolve the National Science Foundation, to require prayer in all public schools, and to privatize national parks. Senator Alan Franklin of Michigan quipped that he planned to add a rider to Way's Sasquatch bill declaring that dinosaurs still exist in America." The anchor introduced Dr. Worthy Dinkle of the National Hurricane Center.

"Sure are interesting times, as the Chinese say, huh, Major?" Moreno said.

"I'm not sure that Franklin realizes that Way would welcome that rider," Blevins said. "Way's a young Earth creationist. Believes dinosaurs co-existed with humans before Noah's flood."

"Idiot. Didn't he go to college?"

"Yeah, but some Christian fundamentalist school, something like New Day College of the Gospel up in the Panhandle, maybe in Vernon. Know who else went there? Our Sheriff Todd."

Moreno put a hand to her forehead. "I wish you hadn't told me that. I already didn't have a whole lot of confidence in our leadership."

"How about this," Blevins said. "His brother was the mayor for a while. Got elected on the promise to bring God back to Marion county schools."

"Did he do it?"

"Resigned after a few months because of a scandal."

"What kind of scandal?"

"An affair with a city employee. The current mayor was the city manager then, and he filled out the term and then won the next election mostly by parading out his five kids and wearing a big gold cross pinned to his lapel."

"I don't even know who our mayor is."

"Young guy named Pitcher. The good news is that Ocala has what's known as a weak mayor. Makes a few appointments, but his power is subordinate to the city council. Bad news is the council is made up mostly of religious nuts. Last year they almost passed a regulation requiring all city employees to be members of a church. It failed by one vote."

"Wait," Moreno said. "Isn't that against the Constitution's religious test clause?"

"Yeah, but that has usually, I believe, been interpreted to apply only to federal employees. Even so, do you think these people give a damn about the Constitution, except for the second amendment?"

"Good God." Moreno stood and walked to the door. She looked down the hall, and then returned to her chair. "Major, how'd you turn out different than most people around here?"

"I reckon in some ways I am." Blevins pushed a button on the bed control to raise it to a seated position and then lowered the sound from the television. "I started as a business major at UF. I was going to take over my father's failing horse farm, but I got interested in philosophy. I got a research assistantship for grad school and was nearly done with my Ph.D. when I decided . . . " Blevins paused. He pressed his thumb to the IV on in his forearm. "Hell, this was over thirty years ago, so what the shit does it matter? Truth is, I plagiarized my dissertation and got kicked out. There. Came home with my tail between my legs and no prospects, so I enrolled in the police academy—I'd taken a couple of criminal justice courses at the College here years before—and took a job here."

"So, you think studying philosophy made you more, um, I guess the word is 'enlightened'?"

"I really need something to drink, and I don't mean water. Hell, I can talk all day with you about the great philosophers— Aristotle, Hume, Nietzsche—well, at least I *could*. I've forgotten a heap of it. I keep saying that when I retire I'll spend my time reading up on those old guys again, but I'm just not sure about the practical effects it had on me. Hell, I find more deep thought in music these days. We had a guy in the department who killed himself by an overdose of Klonopin a few years back. It's an anti-anxiety med."

"Yeah. I heard about it."

"Then somebody gave me a copy of a CD by Jason Isbell, and one of his songs mentioned a friend who'd done the same. Got me interested in a number of young singers in what's known as the Americana genre. Ever heard of Isbell?"

"Don't think so."

"You should listen to him. I think he's the greatest songwriter of his generation."

Moreno shook her head. "You mean his cracker generation."

"OK," Blevins said. "Fair enough. What do you listen to?"

"I like it old school. Prince, Michael Jackson, Lenny Kravitz, Whitney. Shit, I think her song 'I Will Always Love You' might be the best thing I ever heard."

Blevins slid back to draw himself up higher in the bed. "You call that old school? Old school is Chuck Berry, Ray Charles, James Brown, Jackie Wilson, Aretha."

"Damn, Major, this your way to get over some white guilt?"

Blevins laughed. "Think it'd be that easy? By the way, you know that your Whitney song was written by Dolly Parton, right?"

"Hell, now you got to cracker it up. Whoever wrote it, Whitney sang the hell out of it."

"Of course she did," Blevins said. "But did you ever hear Dolly sing it?"

"Goddamn. Let's just agree they're both great, OK?"

"Lighten up, Roberta. We're just talking music, nothing more."

Moreno looked at floor corner as if expecting to find a pest. "Major, it's always something more."

Sheriff Todd walked into the room. "How's it swinging there, Blevins? I tried to get here earlier. You can't believe the shit stack I'm working through, what with Zim Bob here and the media up my ass about the bears and all. Hear me? So you got a busted ticker, eh?"

"Not even dented," Blevins said.

"Let me take a load off there, hon," Todd said to Moreno. Moreno did not respond.

"Deputy," Todd said, "I said I need to sit."

Moreno turned her head up to face Todd. "Pardon me, Sheriff Todd. I must not've notice you come in." She moved from the chair and looked toward Blevins. He smiled.

Todd sat. "How bad is it?"

"Nothing much," Blevins said. "Just heat stroke." He looked

towards Moreno and raised an eyebrow. "They're letting me go home tonight."

"Good, and you're gonna stay home," Todd said. "They told me heart attack. Same difference. Sick leave at least until Thursday. Hear me? Damned if I'll have anybody say I put a man back on duty right after a heart attack. I'm closing this case. Alice will write up the report, then the FDLE can do whatever in the hell they want to with it."

"Good. We've got no leads anyway."

"Then why in holy mother loving to God hell were you out there at Mauser's place, and for shit's sake by yourself?"

"Just following up."

"Deputy," Todd said to Moreno. "How about you run down and get some coffee for all of us." He gave Moreno a five dollar bill.

Moreno rolled her eyes, took the money, and left without speaking.

Todd stood and leaned over the bed until his face was inches from Blevins's. "Listen to me, Blevins. You know I know all about your history with Mingo. When you asked me to let you take on this case, I should've had the sense to see this personal bull shit between you two might blow up. You're not going to make a fool of me. I don't give half a shit about that dead scientist son of a bitch. You take time off, and as far as we're both concerned, this whole damn thing is over. You hear?" Todd jabbed his middle finger onto Blevins's chest where a cardiovascular electrode monitor was taped under the hospital gown. "Shit. I didn't mean to hit that. You OK?"

"I think that made me even better," Blevins said.

"Then I should have tapped it harder." Sheriff Todd sat down. "I didn't want to bring this up, Blevins, but I think I have to. You've got to admit that I've supported you looking for your daughter. Gave you a wide berth to use department resources. Let you contact the FBI. Law enforcement agencies all around the country. Even had Alice and others helping you. I let you to take a bunch of time off to go looking for her a few times. You know I'm not blaming you for any of that. God knows I'd've done the same thing if my daughter'd run off. Hear me? I'll bet you think that I didn't know you went to Starlight camps way off in other states a few times, huh? You must've thought she might've joined up with them. Ain't that right?"

Blevins thought about a trip to the Great Smoky Mountains the previous summer. He stopped to ask directions from a prison crew shoveling asphalt into potholes. A trustee approached his car window, and Blevins asked about a place called Elkmont Cove.

The trustee leaned into the car and looked into the back seat. "You going up the mountain, friend. You need to go down the mountain."

"So, I ought to turn around then, eh, chief?" Blevins asked.

"What'd you call me, motherfucker?" The man opened the car door, grabbed Blevins by the collar, and tried to yank him out of the car, but the safety belt was fastened. Blevins punched the man in the throat. He released Blevins and sank to his knees as others charged the car.

"What the hell's going on?" shouted a man with a badge. He pointed a pistol at Blevins. Two other trustees lifted the gasping man to his feet.

Blevins held up his hands. "I'm with the Sheriff's Department from Mrion County, Florida. My shield's in my pants pocket." The man nodded, and Blevins reached into his pocket and showed his badge.

"Why'd this man attack you?" the officer asked.

The trustee gagged. "Bastard called me . . . ." His voice was thin. "Called me a Chockaraw."

"I have no idea what he's talking about," Blevins said. "I asked for directions, and he told me to turn around. I think."

The man tried to free himself from others who held him. "Called me a Chockaraw, motherfucker!"

"Calm yourself, Redbone," another trustee said.

"Put his ass in the truck," said the officer. He turned to Blevins. "Sorry about this, Major. Some kind of local ethnic slur. I'm not from around here, so I never could quite get straight on it. Now, what brings you up here?"

"Bombardi," Todd said. "You about to pass out?"

"No," Blevins said. "Just thinking. A hunch about those other camps. Didn't pay off any."

"I think it's more than a hunch for you. Now, is that what's been going on? You wanted to be hands on with this case so you could snoop around for her, eh? You know how I feel about personal involvement with cases."

"That's not what's going on, Ash."

Todd leaned back and crossed his arms. "Blevins, you might ought to think about retirement. You've got enough time in. You could devote yourself full time to looking for her. Hear me? Now I got to head back to the office. That girl never brought our coffee, did she? And still got my money." He stood and looked down at Blevins. "You think about what I said." Todd left.

Moreno entered the room with two cups of coffee seconds after Todd walked out. She handed one cup to Blevins.

"Sheriff just left," Blevins said. "If I didn't know any better, I'd think you made sure to miss him.

Moreno sat by the bed. "Then I guess you don't know any better. So, you get the first degree?"

"Naw. He just wanted to make sure I'm OK and say a prayer for me.

"Anything in particular you want me to do while you're off?"

Blevins put his coffee cup on a table by the bed. "There'll be plenty of paperwork to go around with the report. And listen: that Driggers guy doesn't need to be mentioned, but if he shows up again, though I doubt he will, you let me know immediately."

SUMMER 1986

The two weeks at home had not been as unpleasant as Blevins had expected. His parents' fights about money had escalated since the previous summer, but it seemed as if these spats had become a routine in which they took a measure of comfort. Tom had completed a year at the community college while living at home and was accustomed to ignoring the tension and shouting. Blevins even enjoyed working with the horses, and his mother's home cooked meals were welcome relief from a graduate student's cheap fare.

He had considered staying in Gainesville despite receiving no summer money from the university. His research assistantship's meager stipend for the fall and spring semesters was barely enough for his portion of the rent for an apartment that he shared with two other grad students. He subsisted on instant grits for breakfast, olive loaf sandwiches for lunch, and a slice of pizza for most of his suppers. Coffee was free in the philosophy department office, and he had given up smoking to save a few dollars, which meant he could enjoy a couple of beers on weekends. A temporary job may have allowed him to avoid three months at home over the summer break, but he cringed at the prospect of waiting tables or bagging groceries. Besides, he felt an obligation to take some of the pressure of family life off of Tom.

This day had been like any other on the horse farm. The animals need attention, fences and equipment need repairs, and the paddock stalls need constant cleaning. The farm was much smaller than when Blevins was a boy. His father Smiley could train and breed horses, but he could not run a business.

Over the past six years, he had sold more than half his acreage to surrounding farms, and although he started with thirty horses when he moved down from Kentucky twenty-five years before, he now owned only nine.

"Seems like the smaller we get the more work we have to do," Smiley said.

"That's because you don't have all the help you used to," Tom said.

Smiley pointed at Tom with a farrier hammer. "You think I don't know that? It ain't like you're much help neither. And that brother of yours. Seems like when he comes home he's done forgot everything I taught him and has to start over."

"Give him break, Pop. He's a scholar."

"Scholar hell. Here comes your scholar now with his thumb up his ass. I got you ripping up the roads chasing poon every chance you get, and then your mama's on my back all day about wanting to get rid of the whole farm and starting some other kind of business. What am I supposed to do? This is all I know. Let's ask the scholar, huh? What am I supposed to do?"

"I don't know, Pop," Blevins said.

"Must be hell supposed to be a scholar and not knowing anything," Smiley said. A horse whinnied in a nearby stall. "King's had the colic for three days now. Off his feed. I hate to have to get the vet out here again. Still owe him for the last time."

"Pop," Blevins said, "maybe I don't have to go back in the fall. I've already started my dissertation, so technically I don't really need to be on campus. I'll just sign up for some research hours and go in every few weeks to talk to my advisor. That way I could be here and give you some help."

"Help? Help with what—eating up my groceries? You old enough now that I ought to charge you rent. Both of you. I'd already left home and was down here busting my ass when I was Tom's age."

"But you had all that money from Granddaddy when you started," Tom said.

Smiley worked his jaw like a horse chewing a carrot. "One more word, just one more from you, buddy boy. Now get y'all's ass out of my sight and fix that fence like you were supposed to do yesterday."

"I got to run get some more planks," Tom said.

"You always got somewhere to run, ain't you? I swear to goddamnit God I've about had it."

★ ★ ★ ★ ★ ★ ★ ★ ★ ★ ★ ★ ★ ★ ★ ★ ★ ★

They ate supper in silence. Smiley washed down his grits and fried tilapia with gulps from a bottle of Early Times bourbon.

"Help me get this cleaned up, boys," Carolyn, Blevins's mother, said. She reached for Smiley's plate.

"I ain't done," he said. "Get me another one of them fish."

"Ain't no more," Carolyn said. "We've had to cut back on everything."

Smiley rose and left the room. The others were by the table with dishes and glasses in their hands when Smiley returned with a .44 revolver with an eight-inch barrel.

"Time for me to do some cutting back," Smiley said. He raised the gun and pointed it at Carolyn's forehead. She looked at the long barrel with no more concern than horses had when about to be put down by the same weapon. Tom leaped towards his father just as the gun fired. Blood exploded from the back of Carolyn's head and splashed onto the china cabinet that held the good dishes they never used. She plopped down into a chair as if she were resting from a day of hard work. Two plates and a glass settled onto her lap.

Smiley hit Tom on the head with the gun barrel. Blevins was surprised by the sound of the blow, which reminded him of the smack of football helmets. Tom fell to his knees by the table and curled with his face to the floor and his hands on his head. He looked to Blevins as if he were practicing a "duck and cover" drill.

Blevins moved to his mother and squatted beside her. "Mama. Mama."

Carolyn slumped over. Her face pressed against Blevins's chest. The back of her head looked as if it had been scooped out with a post hole digger, exposing lumps of red and gray like a mass of fish guts. She slid from Blevins, bumped against the table, and slumped to the floor.

"Blevins," Smiley said. For an instant Blevins expected his

father to instruct him to load her into the back of the truck. "You wanted to help out? Then call the Sheriff and tell him I'm waiting right here. Goddamnit, that bitch is spiteful even dead. Look—knocked over my liquor."

Blevins and Tom sat on the truck tail gate and watched the horses being loaded into two long trailers.

"I'll die happy if I never see one of those damn beasts again," Tom said.

"You should have called around for more offers, maybe got a better price," Blevins said.

"Didn't you think dealing with probate was enough of a hassle? Last thing I wanted was to haggle with a bunch of bastards like it was a yard sale. I just want them out of here. I've seen too many people killed by those beasts. Mama makes another one."

"That's stupid."

"The hell it is. She was right telling him to quit this damn farm and do something else. Pride. Pride got him in prison and Mama in the ground."

The men from Golden Sun Farms were having trouble getting a stallion into a trailer. The horse yanked on the ropes and bucked. A stocky, dark man behind the horse yelled 'Yah!,' and the animal leaped and kicked him in the chest with both back hooves, sending him tumbling backwards into the mud. The stallion then scampered into the trailer. Two men helped the kicked man to his feet, and he shuffled away wheezing with his arms wrapped around his ribs.

"Looks like Sweet Boy wanted to make one last statement," Tom said. He took a Barlow knife from his pocket, opened it, and scraped mud from the side of his boot. "Like I said last night, we ought to sell the land. Keep an acre and the house. You can live here if you want to. I'm leaving."

"Leaving to where?" Blevins asked.

"I'm going to a monastery up in South Carolina. Spend a year or two getting my head straight."

"You're making no damn sense."

"Makes perfect sense to me. I did some research. This monastery is located right where Mama's people came from, and the monks who started it were from Kentucky like Pop."

Blevins laughed. "So you're going to convert to Catholicism, eh?"

"We kind of are already. Pop was raised Catholic, though he hadn't gone to church in probably forty years. But I don't give a shit about religion. Just want to try the quiet life for awhile, get away from society. You ever read the Tao-te-ching?"

"Now that's an idea, live among Catholic monks but be a closet Taoist. And I don't think you're cut out for celibacy."

Tom wiped his knife blade on the edge of the tail gate. "I can handle it. I've made up my mind. We'll get everything sold off and put the money in the bank. Then I'll hop on a bus and trade these Wranglers and boots for a robe and sandals."

A man in a wide straw hat and red boots approached them. "Got them loaded up, boys. What y'all going to do with that tack and equipment? Most of it's pretty run down, but I'll take it off your hands, make you a good deal on all of it."

"We appreciate it, Mr. Brinson," Blevins said. "We'll let you know."

"Soon," Tom said. "Know a good realtor? We're selling off most of this property."

"My sister's a realtor," Brinson said. "I'll have her give you a call."

The trailers and horses left. Blevins and Tom drove the truck around the pasture to the house. They sat on the porch and watched a red-bellied woodpecker crawl up the trunk of a laurel oak.

"I suppose you're right about selling off most everything," Blevins said. "I could stay here and live off my share of the money from the sale and work on my dissertation. Commute to Gainesville every now and then. When I finish up and get a teaching position somewhere, I'd just as soon sell the house too."

"Sounds good to me," Tom said. "I'm getting me a Jack and Coke. Want one?"

"Already had one. I could stand another."

"Won't be long before I got to make do with just a sip of

communion wine on Sunday. You know, you could rent the house out when you start teaching at Harvard. It's not like you'll be getting rich off a professor's salary. Besides, I might get tired of monking before long and decide to come back. You just never know, do you?"

Blevins nodded. "That's one thing I do know. You just never know."

Fall

The department chair's office contained no books. Dr. Kleinman's allergy to paper—or perhaps dust or mold, Blevins was not sure—kept his face and hands red and peeling. In class he wore latex gloves to turn yellowed pages of Aristotle. Blevins sat before Kleinman's desk with his dissertation advisor, Dr. Weber, seated beside him.

"Rachel," Kleinman said, "would you like to begin?"

Weber rubbed the large, green scarab pendant hanging from her neck by what looked to Blevins like a loop of sisal twine. "We have a dire situation, Blevins, most dire. I fear the outlook may be bleak. There's no easy way to say this. The draft of your dissertation contains a plagiarized passage, a substantial passage."

Blevins felt nauseated.

"I detected a sudden change of style as I read the draft," Weber said, "and with a little research, I found the passage in Langston's *Kierkegaard and the Leap unto Death*, which I have on my shelf. You were careful with all of your other references. Was this just an egregious case of carelessness?"

Kleinman scratched his cheek. "We recognize that this was a draft. Perhaps it was more a matter of sloppy scholarship than intentional deception. Maybe you hurriedly threw together that part of the work to meet your deadline. If so, we may be able to work this out to everyone's satisfaction."

Blevins felt hot and out of breath. His hands shook. Perhaps this was what people meant by an anxiety attack. At the moment, he thought that this physical anxiety was worse than the existential sort Kierkegaard wrote about. "My father murdered my mother this summer. I saw it happen."

Weber leaned over and put her hand on Blevins's forearm. "We know that, and you know we're very sorry. I'm sure this has been a very painful and stressful time for you."

"Are you saying," Kleinman said, "that this was an unfortunate oversight due to stress caused by that . . . horrible episode?"

"Yes," Blevins said. He moved his arm from under Weber's hand. "No. That's not what I'm saying." He took three deep breaths. His racing pulse drummed in his ear. "Working on it kept my mind off of things over the summer. I was able to be distracted from the fact that I was doing my work at the same kitchen table where she died. But as the deadline that I agreed to approached, I just didn't care anymore. The dissertation seemed so worthless, so futile. You know, that old absurdity of life thing." He smiled, but the others did not seem amused.

"I want to understand," Weber said. "Are you saying that this was not a blunder, not sloppiness? Even that would be a great disappointment to me. But if I'm hearing you correctly, you deliberately plagiarized, ignoring the seriousness of it?"

Blevins's nausea subsided. He felt as if a breeze had refreshed his heated face. "That's correct. I know you feel insulted, Dr. Weber, as you should. This was pure deception on my part. I just wanted it over with."

"I appreciate your candor, Blevins," Kleinman said. "Dr. Weber and I will discuss this with Dr. Hertz, who just took over as graduate coordinator, but I have little doubt that the outcome will be anything but removing you from the program."

"Well," Blevins said.

"I just have one question," Weber said. "You're an excellent student and extremely smart young man, Blevins. I'm not only insulted, as you said, but perplexed. Did you really think this would slip by me and the others on your committee, or did you, maybe, want this to happen?"

Blevins tilted his head towards Weber and made a *cluck* with his tongue. "Well, I guess sometimes you just never know."

FEBRUARY, 2018

Boxes of books were stacked on Dr. Somers's floor by the chair where Blevins sat. The books were packed with their spines up: Ludwig Binswanger, R. D. Laing, Rollo May, Viktor Frankl, Otto Rank. Somers leaned over the desk and pointed to a title.

"You might be interested in that one in the corner," Somers said. "*The Book of Tea* by Okakura. A Japanese philosopher, I can't remember his name, said his teacher gave a copy to Heidegger years before he wrote *Being and Time*. He claimed that Heidegger stole one of his central ideas from that book. What was Heidegger's word for human existence?"

"Dasein," Blevins said.

"Yes, dasein. I don't know if Heidegger ever responded, maybe the same way he was silent in his later years about being a Nazi. Take the book, a farewell present. In fact, take any others you want. Most of them have just gathered dust on the shelves these thirty years. I'll probably end up donating them all to the library."

"Thanks," Blevins said. He placed the book on his lap and set his coffee cup upon it. "Heidegger gave an interview to *Der Spiegel* magazine in the mid-sixties, I think, and defended his past actions. Said he cooperated with the Nazis in an effort to keep them from taking over the university but also because of some grand idea of German destiny and the country needing a leader at a crucial historical moment. Nobody bought it."

"I guess he'd had a few decades to rationalize things to his own satisfaction. Oh, before I forget, be sure to sign the form Kristina has for you giving me permission to release your records to Dr. Leland. You're going to get along well with her. She has horses. So, how are we going to wrap things up?"

Blevins blew on his coffee. "I have an ethical issue I'd like to discuss."

"Ethical? You're the philosopher here."

"Well, I guess I need a sounding board, and you're the only person I know who's required to keep secrets."

"Within some rather broad limits."

"I think this falls within those limits. Imagine this: a detective is working a homicide case and comes to suspect that his daughter is responsible. His professional ethics, of course, demands that he arrest her as a suspect. His personal ethics, though, tells him to cover up the whole thing, maybe even pin the murder on someone else."

"Certainly a moral dilemma."

Blevins sipped his coffee. "I think I might miss this coffee more than I'll miss you. Now add to this scenario the fact that the daughter has been missing for years, and this detective sees a chance, maybe, to get her back, to start their lives anew."

"He's also risking his career."

"He doesn't care about his career. He's even willing to lose his retirement pension if it comes to that."

"The way you describe it," Somers said, "I suspect this detective, if he manages to get his daughter and decides that she's in fact guilty of the crime, will cover things up. It sounds to me that his love for the girl trumps any other considerations and that he's already made up his mind. However, he'll likely engage in some extensive rationalization, delude himself into believing that she was innocent all along."

"That's probably only natural, isn't it?"

"Self-delusion in general is natural. We overestimate our abilities, think of ourselves as above average at nearly every task, better than all our work colleagues, consider ourselves at the center of all our friends' lives. When these self portraits get shattered, people come to me for help putting them back together. You could say I'm in the art restoration business."

Blevins smiled. "Life as a work of art. Nietzsche said that's how we should think of our lives."

"I've always said he was more a psychologist than a philosopher," Somers said. "Do you think of yourself as art work?"

"Maybe, but by a pretty bad artist. Could be I've worked with the wrong medium. Switch from marble to bronze, water colors to oils."

"I think that's what our conversations these past two years have been all about. Redefining yourself. Abandoning the wife-killer label."

"Yeah," Blevins said. He ran his thumb along the edge of *The Book of Tea*. The pages were rough cut, which seemed to Blevins to add a note of seriousness to a book. "Rough around the edges."

"How's that?"

"Nothing. Just the book pages. More like real life where nothing's evenly finished."

"Interesting metaphor," Somers said. "Life as a book instead of an *objet d'art*."

"Demands a heap of self-editing."

"Or a second edition."

"Unless it goes out of print."

"We could do this all day," Somers said. "Unfortunately, or, perhaps, fortunately for this tired metaphor, we're out of time." He held out his open palm, and he and Blevins shook hands. "I think you're going to be fine, Blevins. I just hope that detective thinks carefully about what to do with his daughter."

Blevins stood. "I believe you're right. He's probably already made up his mind."

★ ★ ★ ★ ★ ★ ★ ★ ★ ★ ★ ★ ★ ★ ★

Buses, campers, cars, and trucks lined Highway 40 and Baseline Road for miles. Police officers and deputy sheriffs directed traffic while Silver Springs Park rangers shuttled visitors into the park on trailers pulled by four-wheelers. Cloud cover and a steady breeze, harbingers of Hurricane Artemis, provided some relief from the ninety-five-degree heat. Fights broke out, resulting in three arrests, over choice spots for lawn chairs in front of the main stage where country singers in the twilight of their careers had performed years before when "Nature's Theme Park" was a privately owned tourist attraction and the glass-bottom boats floated over cold, artesian springs. The animals—giraffes, Asian bears, lemurs, and a petting-zoo with goats and sheep—were all gone. Most of the hundreds of alligators, fat and black, looking more like bumpy dead logs than living creatures, had been "harvested." Today, though, no one pined for the Jungle Ride through the swamp or wondered how many gallons gushed from the Blue Grotto or cared that what was once called "the world's purest water" was now polluted by fish-killing nitrates from golf course fertilizer, septic tank run off, and waste from the nearby 10,000-acre Aberdeen Cattle Ranch and Abattoir. They were not curious about the meaning of "abattoir." Instead, they thumbed the pocket-sized New Testaments distributed at the gates by members of the Springs Eternal mega-church, listened to hymns from the New Mount Zion Is Here choir, and awaited the appearance of Reverend Possible Pyron.

Blevins watched the crowd amass from the shade of a live oak about a hundred yards from the Twin Oaks Mansion Concert Stage, which was constructed to suggest the portico of an old plantation house. It was draped in red, white, and blue banners and a backdrop announcing "Soldiers of the Lord!" Three young deputies stood in front of the stage, their backs straight and their hands on their belts. Blevins knew how hot those uniforms could be and was glad that he was in "citizen" clothes. He wore shorts, aviator-style sunglasses, a wide jute hat with a green, plastic sun shade on the front of the brim, an untucked fishing shirt with a multitude of pockets and loops and a vented back, and Rockport Easy Walkers. He remembered how Diana called them "old man shoes" and teased him about their Velcro straps. Most of the deputies probably would not recognize him out of uniform, but he suspected that the disguise would not last through the day.

A teenage boy near Blevins passed out firecrackers to friends. Someone should tell them, he thought, that they would get into trouble if they lit them.

The choir left the stage, and a park ranger introduced Mayor Pitcher. The mayor welcomed the crowd, the largest gathering of "good people" the county had ever hosted, he said, and declared the day a "great historical and momentous moment" in which "destiny will be made for the future." The event was one for the books, "not just history books, but the big one in heaven." The audience applauded, and there were shouts of "Praise Jesus!" and "Hallelujah!" A few yards from Blevins a woman raised a Bible over her head and whooped as if she were at a football game. Blevins thought he saw the Florida Gators emblem on the Bible cover.

The speaker system squawked, and Mayor Pitcher stepped back from the microphone. He returned and began his introduction of Senator Robert Way. The volume had been turned up so loudly that Blevins was reminded of a concert by The Who that he had attended nearly forty years earlier and after which his ears rang for three days. He wished he had brought the foam rubber ear plugs he used at the shooting range. When the mayor mentioned the senator's name, nearly everyone chanted "Zim Bob! Zim Bob!" as Way was escorted onto the stage by the North Marion High School JROTC color guard. Four majorettes from Lake Weir High School twirled batons and kicked their tall, white boots. Three members of the Belleview Marching Band pounded two snares and a bass drum. The senator waved and crossed the stage three times so that all could have a good look at him.

"Thank you and amen!" Way said into the microphone as the chanting waned and the students left the stage. "Thank you Mayor Fletcher and to all of you here today, some of you from many, many miles away, on this monumental occasion. I also wish to thank Harvey and Winslow Cain of the Cain Foundation for their assistance with Reverend Pyron's tour and all the great work they do to try to return this country to the vision of our Founding Fathers." Applause, whistles, and "Amen!" erupted from the crowd. A man near the stage held up a United States flag by two corners and flapped it as if he were removing sand from a beach towel. Way stiffened like a soldier at attention and saluted the flag.

"Fellow citizens," Way continued, "we are in the midst of a war, not a war of tanks and jets and bombs and bullets, but a war of the spirit. This great nation has been crippled by godlessness and socialism. We have battles on all fronts, from saving the unborn babies to restoring marriage to the Bible's way to putting God back into schools to using God's green Earth as He intended. Now, as you know, even as I speak Hurricane Artemis is barreling toward us. Did you know that 'Artemis' was the name of a pagan goddess? I guess even the weather men who named it are against us. Now, good people, when has a hurricane ever hit in February? How can you explain it except as God's wrath? I know that the godless listening to this on the radio are laughing at me right now, calling all of us ignorant and backwards for our beliefs." Shouts of "Boo!" arose in the crowd. "That's OK, though. Let them have their fun while they can. They won't be laughing when the mighty hand of God strikes them with hundred-and-fifty mile an hour winds and their roofs go flying off their houses and all their Karl Marx books get washed away!"

The crowd cheered. Several air horns blasted. A man standing beside Blevins poked him in the ribs. "Old Zim Bob's telling it like it is, eh, brother?" His T-shirt read "Crackers for Christ."

Blevins thought the man looked familiar. He may have arrested him in a squabble over a boat motor in Scrambletown years ago. "Yeah. Right on."

Way spread his feet apart and placed his hands on his hips. "Who are the soldiers for right in this war? Politicians? Well, a few, and you know who they are. Our teachers? Maybe the ones who refuse to be strong-armed into joining their socialist union, and durn well not the liberal college professors with their feminism and their post-modernness classes. What about the Supreme Court? Four of them, the ones who know that man's law is second to God's law. We have four other justices, two of them appointed by our previous President," [Boo!] "who practice their 'revisionist law,' and one who is lukewarm and should be, as the Holy Bible tells us, spewed from our mouths. How about the preachers? Many of them, at least the ones who preach the living Word, and surely not those who have welcomed the queers—oh, excuse me—the same-sex partners onto their pews." [Boo!] "But war is won by the common foot soldier. The man, or woman, who volunteers to put his life on the line for the preservation of the American way. Say, maybe I'll change may name to 'American Way.'"

The audience cheered. Blevins felt another poke in the ribs. The cracker for Christ smiled at him.

"It's those who elbow their way ahead to be on the front lines," Way said, "who wins battles and brings home the spoils of war. Now, good people, who are those foot soldiers? You are, good citizens! The salt of the Earth! You, who struggle against a socialist system that takes hard-earned money from your pocket and food off your table. You, who try to show your children the righteous path while the godless lure them astray at every step. You, who know that the soil seized from us by soft socialist fingers needs to be returned to the callused hands of the captains of industry who can put that land to the use as the Holy Bible teaches and as our forefathers so bravely fought the British for so we can live in freedom. Yes, good people, freedom is at stake in this war, and there is no freedom except God's freedom. Who's with me? Soldiers, are you ready to fight?"

The crowd roared and began a chant of "Fight! Fight!" Small United States, Florida's state, and a few "Don't Tread on Me" flags swirled above heads. The horn section of the Vanguard High School band climbed onto the stage and played "Onward Christian Soldiers," and the crowd tried to sing along. Blevins left his shady spot and squeezed through the mass of people, most of whom were standing and clapping to the beat. Visitors still poured in, and he wondered where they all found space to park their vehicles. He caught a familiar scent—someone was smoking pot.

He made his way towards the old giraffe barn, and the smell of pot was replaced by the musky residue of those long-necked and long-gone beasts, much like that of the horse paddocks of his youth. A dozen or more tied-dyed and barefoot Starlights clumped near the fence that had restrained the giraffes, although not enough to prevent their dipping down their great heads to swipe tourists' sunglasses and caps. Blevins recognized several faces and continued on past them towards the carousel that Diana loved to ride when she was a toddler.

She always chose the pink Pegasus and would squeal and yell that she was flying as she spun past Blevins. Sometimes he would toss a kernel of popcorn that she would try to catch in her mouth, and with each year she got bolder, riding without holding the pole, lying across the horse like a wounded cowgirl, calling herself "Running Deer" and pantomiming shooting a bow, standing in the saddle like a circus performer, pretending to take a bullet in the chest and slumping over.

Coming around the carousel were Sergeant Dolens and Deputy Cartwright. Blevins changed direction and sidled through the sweaty crowd towards the front, stepping on empty beer cans and dropped paddle fans with Bible verses and church schedules on one side and advertisements for realtors and bail bondsmen on the other. He ignored the rest of Way's address until the name "Pyron" blasted from the speakers, and the people around him jumped to their feet and cheered. A man beside him threw up his arms, knocking Blevins's hat to the ground. Blevins picked it up, and as he stood and set the hat back on his head, his saw fifteen feet away, the unmistakable, broad back of Mingo Mauser. Beside Mingo was Reverend Campbell, with about thirty other people clustered around them, all of them wearing white T-shirts with "Jehovah: The 2018 Final Tour" on the back.

Blevins tried to flank the group to get a look at them all. He stepped to his right but was blocked by the tightly packed bodies. People behind pushed toward the front, knocking him into a man and woman who did not seem to mind being jostled. He felt hands on his shoulders—a short woman was using him for leverage as she jumped to try to peer over him.

"The time is ripe, brothers and sisters," Pyron's voice boomed. "Ripe for Victory! Victory over the forces of Satan that have taken our country and are trying now to take our souls. But we, the soldiers of the Lord, say 'No, you will go no further.' We watched as Satan's demons kicked God out of our schools. We watched as the demons walked hand in hand with the Islam jihadists who want to kill us all. We watched as our socialist government snatched property away from hard-working farmers and turned it into federal land. Fertile land where we could build our homes and our churches, where we could raise our cattle and our hogs, where we could nurture by the word of God our children and our grandchildren. Land that holds God's riches that he gave to the American people centuries ago. Land swelling with oil waiting to be freed so that we are not at the mercy of the Islam Arabs every time we crank up our cars and trucks."

The crowd cheered for each of Pyron's announcements. Blevins wondered if they were even listening and would cheer for anything the preacher said. The woman behind Blevins stopped jumping but still gripped his shoulders. Between the heads in front of him, he got a peek at Pyron: tan suit, bald head, wide, red face.

Pyron removed the microphone from the stand and stood at the front edge of the stage. "Land's not all they're interested in taking. They want to take our faith, too. Fifty-some years ago, they took prayer out of our schools. Now, they'll say to you, 'Your children can pray anytime they want to, it just can't be a school prayer.' Well, I say, 'Then what is a school for if it's not about the truth?' But you know what, brothers and sisters? They don't care about the truth. They say that Adam and Eve aren't the truth. They say that millions and millions of years ago humans come from monkeys. We were swinging from the trees, and the next thing you know we're planting corn and building cities. You know what they call it. They call it evolution. Well I call it devilution! You want truth? I'll ring in the truth, because I am the Lips of the Lord and a truth in-ringer!"

The woman released Blevins so that she could clap her hands. The white T-shirt group began chanting "Devilution!" and others joined in.

Pyron wagged his head and slid a few feet across the stage in James Brown fashion. He pulled off his suit jacket and threw it to the back of the stage. "Truth in-ringer! Now, they'll hide behind the name 'scientist' and say they have proof. They say they've got millions of fossils they dug up in Africa that prove that we come from monkeys. Transitional species, they call them. I know that we've got plenty of dirt diggers here among us today. What truth have you ever found in the dirt? You know what I get when I dig in the dirt? Dirty hands!"

More cheers. Pyron dropped his arms to the side and ducked walked like Chuck Berry back to center stage. "Now I've been following the news here in Florida. Most of you probably know about one of those so-called scientists who was out here in the woods, in some of that federal land, looking for one of those monkey men that's supposed to be a missing link between us and the animals. A big foot, skunk ape as you call it down here. Well, guess who went missing. The missing link hunter himself. Here's something you won't hear on the news: the same thing happened to five more of those fellows out West in the past three months. What does that tell you about what God thinks of them and their missing link?"

Blevins thought these blatant lies were too risky even for a showman like Pyron. How could these thousands of people here believe this nonsense so easily?

Pyron loosened his checkered tie and rolled up his white shirt sleeves. "Truth in-ringer! You brothers and sisters from out of town might not have heard about the bears and monkeys that have been, as the reporters say, 'mysteriously' killed lately. Seventy-seven bears and two-hundred monkeys with arrows shot right through the head. If that's not the angel of the Lord's work, then I don't know what is."

The crowd was beginning to tire, and many settled into their lawn chairs. Mingo and his bunch remained standing. Blevins took a few steps to his left through a row of chairs for a better look at them.

"Truth in-ringer! Brothers and sisters, let me ask you this: You know where AIDS come from? I know what you're thinking—it comes from the homosexual abominators, the sodomites. Well, you're right about that, but that's not the whole truth. It's been medically proven, a scientific fact—yes, there are some of those—that it come from monkeys over in Africa. I don't know how it got from the monkeys to the Africans, but somebody must have been up to another kind of abomination, if you know what I mean. This is the same place where those devilutionists tell us that we came from monkeys. Does that make sense to you? Monkeys give people a death-dealing disease, but they are supposed to be our real ancestors, not Adam and Eve. I'm here to tell you, there weren't any AIDS in the Garden of Eden!"

Pyron kicked around and spun in something resembling an Irish jig. The people who had just sat leaped to their feet again, blocking Blevins as he tried to move further around Mingo's group.

Pyron bent over and panted into the microphone. He wiped a handkerchief across his shiny pate. "Ringing in the truth can be some hard work, brothers and sisters." He stood and moved his extended arm in an arc as if smoothing over the crowd. "So the next thing you know these woods out there are full of monkeys. Did you know that this county has the highest rate of AIDs in the country? Either our doctors can't cure it or they don't want to, but a few arrows from the angel of the Lord can do something about it."

Blevins was surrounded by nodding heads and "Amens." Could all of these people really accept this crooked line of thought as valid?

Pyron dabbed his face with the handkerchief. "How about those bears? You won't get the authorities here to admit it, but I have it from a reliable inside source that twenty-two people have been killed out in those woods by bears in the past year. That's more than died from gunshot. They'll tell you all about the gun deaths, and you know why. The socialists in our government are drafting a law right now to take our guns. Is it because they want to make things safer on the street? No. It's because they know that soldiers for the Lord like you and me are preparing for the revolution! A revolution of revelation! A revolution of righteousness from God's mighty militia!"

A *pop* sounded from the back of the crowd. Probably a firecracker, Blevins thought, but on any other day people would have scattered, thinking it was gunfire. Perhaps they believed it was something planned to mark the revolution. He stretched and looked in the direction of the noise to see if deputies were on the move, but the mass of bodies was too thick.

"So we see," Pyron said, "that no good comes from federal land. Hundreds of thousands of acres, millions and millions more across this once-great country, just laying there, the wasted spoils of socialism. I am thankful that the good people

of this great state had the sense, the faith, to elect a man like
Senator Bob Way, who has dedicated himself to giving those
rich lands to creative and resourceful men who will wrest from
that good earth the treasures the Lord has put there. I close my
eyes, and I can see the bountiful harvest, a feast for the faithful,
and I can hear the voice of God saying to us, 'Well done, my
children. Well done.' Are you hungry for that feast, brothers
and sisters? Will you sup from the table of the Lord?"

Thousands of voices rang out "Yes!" These people have to get
hoarse sooner or later, Blevins thought. Did they think that if
enough conservative politicians would join forces to privatize
all federal lands that they, these regular working people—mechanics, roofers, school teachers, grocery store clerks, short
order cooks, house painters, bait shop owners—would profit
from it, get forty acres and a Husqvarna riding lawn mower?

Pyron rubbed his handkerchief around his neck. "Whoo,
mercy! Hot as the Devil's kitchen out here today. They say it's
suppose to get up to a hundred and ten. When's the last time
you been this hot around Valentine's day? And don't say it was
in 1979 in the back of a Chevelle Malibu!"

Laughter erupted. Blevins saw two women put their hands
over their mouths. A man beside him said, "I ain't believing he
said that!"

"Just a little humor, folks" Pyron said. "The good Lord likes
a joke, too, or why else did he create us so that we can't scratch
our own backs? At least today he gave us a few clouds to block
the sunlight or we'd all be keeling over with the heat stroke by
now. My old punkin head would be one fat red blister. And that
little breeze ain't much, but it helps a little, and I'm thankful for
it. Thing is, we know why those clouds and that breeze are here.
Old Hurricane Artemis is headed this way. Like the senator
said a while ago, you can call a storm a natural happening if
you want to, but in February, that's an act of God. What they
should have named it was Hurricane Abaddon. How many
of y'all know who Abaddon is? He's the angel of destruction
in the Book of Revelation. That's him spinning and blowing
over the Atlantic, sucking up fuel from the Gulf Stream,
drawing a bead on the Ocala National Forest. They say it'll be

up to two-hundred mile-an-hour winds by the time it makes landfall."

A quick gust of wind sent church pamphlets and baseball caps flying over heads. Blevins grabbed the brim of his hat just in time to keep it from becoming airborne.

"Feel that, brothers and sisters?" Pyron asked. "That's just the pinky tip of God's mighty hand. Praise him. Multiply that by about twenty and that's what it'll be like right here in a day or two. God is taking back what was his in the first place, what he promised and bequeathed to us. Our land to live on. Our timber to build houses. Our underground fresh water to drink. Our birthright! That's what we're fighting for!"

Blevins wondered if Pyron was going to get around to drawing a concrete link between this revolution, and whatever action it demanded, to this angry God's hurricane. Would the storm clear a path for the foot soldiers to follow? Would the tempest kill the socialists and sodomists (and probably Catholics and Mormons as well) and save the faithful who could then defend this wholly privatized country against the Muslim onslaught? Blevins was at least sure that Pyron would not say "tempest," which would sound too much like "temptress" to this crowd and create confusion or a more complicated metaphor.

Another sound like a gun shot, this time louder, came from the west side of the park. Blevins managed a couple of steps but could see no activity in the direction of the shot. If his colleagues—Who was in charge out here today? Major Wilkins?—had any reason to think those were shots, they would have started emergency security measures by now. He placed his hand on his hip and felt through his shirt tail the Walther CCP.

A majorette mounted the stage and gave Pyron a bottle of water. He gulped down the entire contents and tossed the bottle into the crowd. A small scuffle ensued over the souvenir. "Bless you, young sister. Friends," he pointed in the direction that the girl had taken to leave the stage, "yonder goes our future. I cannot tell you how much I have been impressed by the strong, young sisters who are leaping into this fight. Some of them are doing as much as the young brothers to lead the battle. Friends, I want to tell you a story."

Pyron walked to the front of the stage, untied and slipped off his shoes, and sat on the edge of the stage. "A few months ago, a young woman joined my flock. She was a runaway from a troubled home. A terrible tragedy had occurred a couple years before, and her heart was broken, and her mind was in a mess. She had no money in her pockets, and no faith in her soul, because her parents had long turned their backs on God and had never exposed her to the Word."

A woman beside Blevins said, "Umm *um*" and shook her head. Her auburn and blond highlighted hair waved over her freckled shoulders. Blevins looked past her back to Mingo's group. He could see Mingo in profile. Was that a black-haired girl on the other side of him?

"This lost young lady said to me," Pyron said, "she said, 'Reverend, I have travelled across this country and back again, looking for some relief for my tortured heart, but nothing has given me satisfaction. I have done some shameful things, all because I desperately wanted to feed my empty soul, to still my trembling heart, but I found no relief. One night, Reverend, I was crashing at a cheap motel with a few other people—I hardly even knew them, just some other runaways like me— and when the others fell asleep, I put a razor blade to my wrist. I asked, Why not? What do I have to live for? I didn't even know who I was talking to, just words in the lonely night.'"

Pyron pulled off his socks and threw them over his shoulders. "Pardon me, friends. I'm just a country boy, and when I get hot, I just got to go barefoot." He stuck out his bare feet and the crowd cheered. A man near Blevins slipped off his cowboy boots and held them high and whooped.

"Brothers and sisters, this was a beautiful young woman. I could tell right away that she was very smart but also that she was in need. Her soul was crying out. She said to me, 'Reverend Pyron, just as I was about to press that razor into my vein and end it all, you came on the television. The music started and the singers were saying you are loved and God knows you better than you know yourself and he needs you and all that, and I thought, well, why not listen for a minute? Then you started preaching about how so much is wrong in our country, in our society, and in our world. How the forces of evil have taken over at every level, at the federal, the state, the county, the town, the subdivision, the family. And I started thinking that maybe everything I thought before wasn't the truth, that what my secularist parents had fed me was a lie, that maybe there is something bigger to believe in, and I thought, hey, it ain't my fault! I didn't cause that terrible tragedy in my family, and even if I did, there is redemption for the soldiers of the Lord!'"

Blevins tried to press forward so that he could see around Mingo. He wedged his shoulder between a man and woman.

"Hey, dude!" a man shouted into his face. "You spilled my Heineken!"

Blevins ignored the man and tried to take another short step between him and the woman.

"Didn't you hear me, motherfucker?" the man said. He was much taller than Blevins, and he leaned down to his press his face against Blevins's hat and peer through the green, plastic brim. His eyes were bloodshot, and his breath smelled like sardines. "You owe me two dollars, or I'm going to fall over you like the wrath of God."

Blevins fought the impulse to punch the man's larynx that jutted out like a pecan. Instead he lifted his shirt tail to reveal his pistol.

The man's eyes widened, and then he smiled and clasped Blevins left hand with both of his. "Aw now, I was just fucking with you, brother. Hey, how about a beer?" He bent over to the cooler by his side and took out a bottle. "Here you go, brother. That'll help you beat this heat."

Blevins took the beer and nodded. The man stepped away a few inches to widen the path, but Blevins saw that he could not go forward through the dense clot of people ahead. Perhaps he could circle back to get a glimpse on Mingo's far side. He backed out the small gap and tried to listen to Pyron.

". . . and the other evils besetting our country. Then we knelt down together and prayed a great long prayer. When we said our amens, she said, 'Brother Pyron, I will be the best warrior for the Lord you have ever seen. I have the weapons, and I knew when I was a little girl that I was training for a purpose, and now you have shown me that purpose. Tell me what God wills of me.' That beautiful young sister spent a month in our Dedication Camp up in Florence South Carolina that the blessed Cain brothers built for our ministries—Brother Way spent some time with us there—and now she's among us today and has been on the front line of the battlefield. I'm not going to ask her to join me up here, because she's a little shy and prefers to work behind the scenes, but let's show her how much we appreciate her faith and strength and courage!"

The audience applauded and whooped. Blevins slipped along a line of chairs, keeping his eye on the towering head of Mingo Mauser. Another gust of wind rushed across the park. Long black hair streamed out beside Mingo.

Pyron stood. "Now brothers and sisters, we have a special guest here today, a local boy who's been doing the Lord's work and reaching millions with his wonderful films. I'm sure you all know Corey Clayton—"

Pow pow came from behind. That *had* to be a rifle, Blevins thought. Someone screamed near the stage. Blevins saw deputies down front rushing about: one jumped the short fence and into the crowd; two others ran to where Pyron sat. People leaped from their chairs and tumbled over each other. A voice came through a bull horn, but Blevins could not tell what was said. "Up there!" someone yelled, and Blevins saw hands pointing to a tree. Two deputies fought their way towards him from his left. Blevins looked up into the tree. Is that a person hunched on a limb? He tried to get closer, shoving bodies and getting shoved. He glimpsed two more deputies on his right. He pointed into the tree. He took his pistol from its holster. A *pow* came from the tree. He raised his pistol and was tackled to the ground. With his face in the grass, he heard more gunfire and screaming. Someone stood on his right hand while some-one else was on his back and shouting into his ear.

"I'm Major Bombardi," Blevins said.

"What? Oh shit," said the person on his back. "Major, what—"

"Get the hell off me!"

The deputies released him, and Blevins got to his feet. Four deputies stood around the base of the tree. Voices from two bull horns instructed people to move calmly toward the gates. Mayor Pitcher was on the stage saying that everything was under control and that people should make way for the Fire and Rescue truck coming through the park.

"Somebody shot that preacher," Deputy Hendricks said to Blevins. "Sorry I took you down. I didn't recognize—"

"Forget it," Blevins said. "You were doing your job. Looks like the shooter was taken out."

"Yes, Sir," Hendricks said. "And some kids were shooting firecrackers earlier. I wonder if they were part of a distraction."

"Could be," Blevins said. He looked around for Mingo and his white-tee-shirts group but did not see them. "I've got to go."

Most of the crowd was bunched at the gates. Lawn chairs, coolers, aluminum cans, and religious tracts, littered the grounds. Blevins saw a few Starlites putting things, probably beers, into their knitted shoulder bags. Deputies questioned people, among them the boy Blevins had seen with the firecrackers. None of Mingo's associates were in sight. Blevins found Major Wilkins with two other deputies near the main gate.

"Blevins?" Wilkins said. "Didn't expect to see you here."

"Just enjoying the show. Any ID on the shooter?"

"Driver's license said Grady Clayton. We think it was that actor kid's father. Maybe he blamed Pyron for his son throwing away his career and turning into a religious fanatic. We picked up another guy with a nine millimeter in his belt, but we don't know if he's connected."

Blevins fished a pill from his shirt pocket and swallowed it. "We need to interview Pyron's people, find out who the rival groups are. You know, the my-apocalypse-is-better-than-yours sorts. Todd here?"

"No. He's with Emergency Operations."

A few yards away a gray-haired woman with a metal walking cane, the kind with the four, rubber-tipped feet at the bottom, yelled at a deputy. "One of you sheriffs shot the Reverend! God will punish you all!" The deputy said something to her and wagged his finger at her face. She swung her cane at the deputy who blocked it and twisted the woman's arm behind her back. She screamed and fell.

"Oh, hell," Wilkins said. "Just what I need." He ran to the scuffle.

Blevins followed the crowd into the parking lot where vehicles jammed and horns blew. He had little hope that he would spot Mingo's truck, but he searched for nearly an hour. Outside the park, cars, trucks, and buses crawled along State Road 40 as far as he could see. Blevins wondered if Pyron's being shot would scare some of these people away from this so-called revolution or if it would convince them even more that the movement had divine backing. If Pyron died, he would surely be transformed into a martyr. Funny, Blevins thought, what a bullet can accomplish.

★ ★ ★ ★ ★　★ ★ ★ ★ ★　★ ★ ★ ★ ★

At 8 PM Blevins sat in his truck at Mingo's house for the third time that evening and had a long pull of whiskey. Again, no one was there. Both Reverend Campbell's house and the church were empty. In between these Forest trips he had gone home, first to change out of his sweaty clothes and next for a meal of bourbon and Vienna sausages on saltines. On the Weather Channel he had seen that seven out of eight computer models showed the hurricane passing through Marion County. Perhaps the members of Mingo's church had fled the storm. Maybe they rendezvoused with other Pyron mourners when they heard that he had died on the way to the hospital. Wherever they were, Blevins was sure Diana was with them. One of Pyron's officers may have declared her work here done, and she could already be on her way to point her arrows at wolves in Yellowstone or grizzlies in Alaska.

He slid the Walther from its holster and aimed over the steering wheel at Mingo's front door. He repelled the bourbon-driven urge to get out of the truck and shoot out a window. Instead, he placed the gun barrel into his mouth. The 9 mm did not have the comfortable fit of the .45. An inelegant way to go, he thought, with the mounting rail digging in behind his top teeth.

If he left now, he could be in Tampa before 10 PM.

The Famous Venus Mound Lounge did not look so famous on a weeknight. The dozen solemn, middle-aged men around the stage appeared more entertained by the three young soldiers than they were by the dancers who knew they would make little in tips from such a small crowd and so did hardly more than shake their asses in each man's face, pick up a few dollar bills, and leave for backstage to await their next unenthused turn. The soldiers were lively, toasting each other repeatedly, buying rounds for the house, and calling all the girls hot mamas. They were probably underage, Blevins thought, but no strip joint in Tampa would refuse servicemen who in all likelihood were shipping out for Syria in the morning.

"Some good old American aaaaass!" one of the soldiers yelled. "That's what I'm talking 'bout!" He and his buddies clicked their glasses and stood to salute the exiting dancer as they had done all the others before her.

"You're looking lonely there, darling," a woman said to Blevins. She wore a bikini bathing suit and high heels and smelled like baby oil. "How about if I join you? I could use a drink."

"No thank you. Is Ophelia here?"

"Who?"

"I mean Cicelia."

The woman sat and put her hand on Blevins's shoulder. "I think so, but she's not dancing tonight. Did you want a private show? I could do that for you."

"Could you please say that Blevins needs to speak to her? Or Harry." He handed the woman a five dollar bill.

"You want to speak to Cicelia or Harry?"

"No. She's knows me as either Blevins or Harry."

"And you know her as either Cicelia or Ophelia. Am I getting this right?"

Blevins gave her another five. "You've got it."

The woman left as the emcee introduced "Maybelene from Abilene, who proves that everything really is bigger in Texas. Giddy up, Maybelene!" A tall woman in a white cowboy hat and boots and sporting tremendous tits emerged from the velvet curtains. She circled the stage and then removed her fringed, sequined vest. Silver, star-shaped pasties covered the nipples of her gargantuan breasts.

A man in his seventies stood and shouted to the soldiers, "Those things look like Howitzers!"

The soldiers did not acknowledge the remark, and Blevins wondered if the boys knew what the man was talking about.

One of the soldiers leapt to his feet. "I'm from Lubbock! Take me home, my long tall hot mama!"

Maybelene stopped in front of the Texan soldier, removed a pasty, and stuck it to the boy's forehead.

"Right between the eyes!" another soldier said.

Maybelene peeled off the other pasty and tossed it to a patron. She extended one arm as if holding reins, slapped an ass cheek, and pretended to ride a horse around the stage as her gigantic boobs flopped up and down, sometimes in unison, sometimes separately.

"Lord, let me be a saddle tonight!" said the Texan soldier.

When her ride was done, she picked up a few bills from the floor, stuffed them in a boot, and waved goodbye with her hat.

"Looks like Maybelene's heading back to the stable, boys," the emcee said. "Now don't go anywhere. Havana Hannah's coming out in a minute to show you how it's done in the Caribbeee-yan!"

The woman who had approached Blevins was back. "Cicelia's about done packing, but she says she's got a minute or two for you."

"Thank you."

"Come find me later. OK, darling?"

"Well."

Blevins found Ophelia where they had their private sessions many times over the past couple of years. She was sitting on the couch and stuffing a white bathrobe into a pink duffle bag.

"Well, Officer Blevins. I didn't expect you here tonight, but you're just in time to help me tote this stuff out to my car."

"The other night when you said you were leaving here, I didn't think you meant this soon."

"This hurricane. I told you about my daughter in Jacksonville, right? I need to get her out of there right away. If that storm turns even a little bit north, Jacksonville's going to get hit hard. I've got a sister up in Spartanburg. We'll head up there. Probably stay. My daughter could use a change. God knows I can, too." She patted the couch.

Blevins sat beside her. "Don't you have other things to get, furniture, whatever?"

Ophelia lit a skinny, black cigarette. "Everything I want is packed in my car already. I just had to run in here a minute for my outfits and make up. I'm not sure why I even came to get them. Not like I need them anymore."

"Maybe an old friend might drop in on you for a private dance some time."

"Will that old friend be you?"

"No. That's why I came to see you." He took the gold-plated lighter from her hand, thumbed it open, lit it, and closed it. "I was trying to come to a decision about something. Something important. I needed to talk it out with you."

"Let's see. So once again your high-priced shrink couldn't help you, right?"

"Well, yeah. I mean, yeah, I think he did."

"But you needed a woman's perspective."

"Maybe. Not just any woman." Blevins raked the lighter across his twill, khaki pants, trying to light it in one motion like he practiced as a kid. He failed. "Now that it looks like I won't see ever you again, I think I've made my decision."

Ophelia laughed. "This means that either I'm one hell of a counselor or you had your mind made up before you got here. This is about your daughter, isn't it?"

"Yes." He read the inscription on the lighter: *To Thine Own Self Be True.*

The door opened, and Maybelene from Abilene entered, pulling the Texan soldier along by the hand. "Cicelia, hon, you about finished? I have a date with this handsome cowboy here."

"Sure, May," Ophelia said. "Grab that bag for me, Harry, and follow me out to the car."

"Take care of yourself, Cicelia," Maybelene said. "You've been like a mama to me."

"Just what I needed to hear," Ophelia said.

Outside behind the Venus Mound Ophelia opened the back of her Corolla. Blevins put the duffel bag in where several other bags lay. In the back seat he could see more bags, books, a sewing machine, and a telescope.

"You're a star gazer?" he asked.

"Used to be. Been working most nights lately, remember? I'm taking it for the grand kids." She leaned against the side of the car and looked up. "Show them the planets, constellations. Maybe if I can teach them how to find their way around at night by the stars it'll help them chart their lives better than I did mine. Tried to do that with my daughter, but she didn't listen too well. How about your daughter? You teach her how to find her way around?"

Blevins closed the car trunk. "I taught her everything I could. Read to her every night. Plato, Descartes, even your Bard. Took her hunting, fishing, camping. She was an expert shot, not just with guns but bow and arrow and sling."

"Ha ha! 'Slings and arrows of outrageous fortune.' Maybe the Shakespeare you read her took hold deep in her subconscious in an odd way."

Blevins smiled. "Maybe. She was some kind of girl. Really grew into her name. Diana. You know, like the Roman goddess of the hunt?"

Ophelia took her key ring from her purse and twirled it around her index finger. "Something must have stuck. Last time you said you thought she'd come back. Not every girl her age can run away for that long and survive."

"I never doubted she'd survive. I wanted her to flourish. I wanted so much more for her. I could have done more."

"You're getting maudlin now," Ophelia said. She stepped in front of him and pointed at him with something on her key ring. "Listen closely. I'm going to get my daughter and take her away. You're going to do the same. Find her, throw her in the car. Handcuff her if you have to. Get her far away, far from everything that's familiar. Isn't that what you were planning?"

Blevins focused on the key ring. A black cylinder a half inch in diameter and about five inches long dangled from it.

"Kubotan. That's good. More women need to know how to protect themselves."

Ophelia put her hands on her hips and laughed. "Jesus Christ! Do you hear yourself, the wife killer? For fuck's sake!"

"That stings."

"I see you didn't listen to me last time and instead went with that quack shrink. Typical man, choosing denial over acceptance. Maybe you should try a little Buddhism, Blevins. It's all about letting go, but you can't let something go that you don't first have. You want to shake off the wife killer identity? Then first you have to make it yours. Tell me this. What do you do when someone asks you if you killed your wife? I'll bet you mumble some spineless thing like, 'It was an unfortunate accident.' Right?" She turned and leaned back against the car beside him. "You want to be somebody else? You've already practiced it as Harry instead of Blevins, and I know there's a lot more about you that you haven't told me. So how about this as the new Blevins—daughter saver? Here's a deal you can make with yourself. First you identify with wife killer, and only then can you trade that in for daughter saver. Make sense? A kind of Buddhist bargain with an existentialist twist."

Blevins took a flask from his hip pocket and offered it to Ophelia.

She took a swig. "That's good bourbon. You have expensive taste for a cop. And only a cop would risk bringing his own liquor into a strip joint."

He had a swallow. "This is no joint. This is the Famous Venus Mound Lounge. Aren't all the drinks here top shelf?"

"You're changing the subject again. Give me another shot." She drank from the flask and wiped her mouth with the back of her hand. "You know, you're one fucked up individual. If we'd started this open-heart confessional bleeding back when you first started coming to see me, I think I could have you straightened out by now."

Ophelia put her arms around his shoulders and pressed her face into the hollow of his neck. "You probably know this, but you're the closest thing I've had to a relationship in a long time. Don't get excited—the last thing I need is a relationship. Point is, for the past few months I've looked forward to your visits. I hate to say this, but I'm going to miss you." She pulled her face away from his neck and looked him in the eye. "Don't let it go to your head. Now, you have to promise me two things. Are you listening?"

"Yes."

"First, you will never try to find me. Context is everything, Blevins. Outside of the lounge, it'd be like we were speaking different languages. Ha! We're *outside* of the lounge now, but this doesn't count." She put her head on his chest. "I know you understand. Everything is about context. If I learned nothing else from studying literature, that's it. Now, second. You will find your daughter, and you will do something big. Maybe you'll take her away. Maybe have her committed. Or just arrest her and let the system do its work. But we both know that you will never rest, you will never be free from the threat of suicide, if you don't do *something*, something that will change both your life and hers."

Ophelia pulled away and tapped Blevins's chest with the kubotan. "Promise me now."

Blevins took her hand into both of his. He thought about kissing the back of her fingers, but changed his mind. "Yes. I promise, although the first one's a shame. I'll never meet another woman like you."

"You don't think I know that? A Shakespeare-quoting, exotic dancer who counsels suicidal cops? I think I've got a monopoly on that niche. Just got to figure out how to market my services." She pulled her hands from his and opened the driver's door. "Now don't get maudlin again. We both have the clock against us. Let's go."

She slid into the driver's seat, cranked, and left without looking back.

Blevins looked up through a gap in the night clouds at a cluster of stars that he thought to be the Pleiades but was not sure. He tried to remember the Greek myth, something about seven goddesses. Maybe Atlas was their father. Maybe they were attendants to Artemis. He was almost sure that they were pursued by Orion, whose constellation looks as if it is chasing them across the night sky. He reached into his pocket and pulled out the gold-plated lighter. *To Thine Own Self Be True.* What a pile of shit, he thought.

AUGUST, 2017

"I just don't understand why we got to come out here in the middle of the night," Maia said. "And a big-ass storm coming up. You know how lightning scares me."

"You don't have to understand it," Mingo said. "He told me to pick it up whenever I want to. This is when I want to."

Maia threw a Miller bottle out of the truck window. "I'm beginning to think you hadn't bought it at all. Just hook up to it and haul it off. Sell it quick. Easy money."

"Think whatever you want."

"You take too many chances, Mingo."

"I took one hell of a chance on you. Still not sure if it paid off."

She punched him on the shoulder. "Watch how you talk. You know damn well you love the shit out of me. You'd fall apart in the floor if I left you."

"Maybe I'd fall back together."

"Shit."

Mingo pulled onto a narrow drive that crossed a ditch and ended before a wide metal gate. He left the truck's engine running with the headlights shining on the gate as he fumbled in the tool box in the truck bed until he found the bolt cutters. He walked to the gate, cut through the padlock, and flung the gate doors open. He returned to the truck and began to drive across the bumpy field.

"So this guy says 'just come over and cut the lock and let yourself in, huh?" Maia asked.

"He give me a key, but I lost it. I'll buy him another lock. They cheap."

"You must take me for a goddamn idiot. And who parks their

boat in the middle of a field? Son of a bitch must be crazy as you are. Was that thunder?"

Mingo made a U-turn and backed the truck toward the boat, a twenty-foot Boston Whaler with a center console.

"That looks like a salt-water boat," Maia said. "I guess you expect me to believe you gonna start fishing for grouper, huh?"

"Just take that flashlight and go guide me back."

"Why you want to involve me in this shit? You know this makes me an accomplice or maybe an accessory, I don't know which is which. Both'll get me time."

Mingo took Maia's hand. "I wanted to show you how much I love you. Do something big together."

"You gonna still love me after five to ten in separate jail cells?"

Maia climbed down from the truck and stood by the trailer tongue. She waved him back, pointed to the left, then flattened her palm as if as if saluting a foreign flag. Mingo waited, but Maia gave no further direction. He put the truck in park and got out.

"What you stop me for?" Mingo asked. He felt a tingling sensation, like his skin was crawling. He looked at Maia. Her long, blonde hair fanned out from her head like rays of light. Then, the explosion.

Mingo was blown from the ground and crashed onto his back. He had never heard a sound so loud. His ears felt as if they had been popped by cupped hands like boys used to do when he was a kid. His lungs were deflated, and his chest hurt. His breath returned after a few seconds. His feet felt as if they were on fire. He smelled burning hair.

He pulled off his smoking shoes. The rubber soles were split apart and melting.

He called for Maia and realized that his hearing was gone except for a humming noise. For a moment he wondered if the lightning strike had somehow started the boat motor.

He saw Maia clumped on the ground fifteen feet from the truck. The flashlight, still shining, lay by the boat tongue where she had dropped it. Mingo was dizzy, but he got the flashlight and crawled around the boat to Maia. She looked as if her clothes had been cut with a razor from the neck of her T-shirt to the right side and from the waist of her jeans down the right leg to the ankle and as if a trench of flesh had been scooped out with a trowel, all the way down her body, and then the wound had been burned with a blowtorch. Smoke came from the black line in her flesh. Her torn shirt had fallen open. Her nipples were as hard as roofing tacks. Her flip flops were gone, and her right foot was completely black.

Mingo touched his fingers to the black line just below Maia's hip bone. The skin was hot and felt like a pork crackling. He called her name four times, but she did not move. Her open eyes looked upward as if studying the source of her death.

★ ★ ★ ★ ★ ★ ★ ★ ★ ★ ★ ★ ★ ★ ★

"When they turning you lose?" Shaky asked.

"Probably tomorrow," Mingo said. He raised the hospital bed to sit up. "Doctor said I had a minor heart attack, now my heart's beating out of time. He said I have to get that back on track."

"How about your ears?"

"About half. Said my hearing ought to be back to normal in a couple of days."

Shaky ate a spoonful of chocolate pudding from the tray on the table by Mingo's bed. "Eeeyo. These hospital eats ain't bad. I don't know how you don't like this pudding."

"I told you. That lightning knocked out my taste. Doctor said he'd never heard of that before."

"That's a shame. Shame about Maia too."

Mingo turned on the television with the remote. "The day I was born my old man was struck by lightning. Didn't kill the old bastard. One of a heap of unlucky near misses in my sorry ass life. Maia too. Why'd she die but not me? By the fucking way, you don't look too shook about her."

"Well, she was just my stepmother, not like blood. She told me the other day she'd about got you to marry her. I guess that would make you my second cousin and my stepfather. Wouldn't that've been some shit? Hieyoo."

"First of all, she was full of shit, because no way I was making that mistake again. Second of all, that wouldn't make me no kind of step anything to you."

Mingo changed the television from the hospital information channel to one showing a rerun of *Friends*. He changed the channel again.

"Hey," Shaky said, "I like that show."

"Bunch of spoiled brat whiney assholes," Mingo said. "They have no idea how good they got it. They ought to be thankful."

"I bet you're thankful you weren't standing where Maia was."

Mingo looked at Shaky for several seconds. "That's all I've been thinking about. That and her being dead. But it could've been me. Makes you wonder."

"About what?"

The infomercial touted a tropical fruit extract that promised to change one's life.

"About life, death," Mingo said. "Why her and not me? Is God trying to tell me something?"

Shaky licked the last trace of pudding from the plastic spoon. "God? I ain't never heard you say not a damn word about God."

"Never really thought much about it. Just didn't ever seem to make no difference to me. I've been through a bunch of shit, but nothing ever hit me like this. It's not like having a deputy sheriff shooting at you and the bullets hitting the wall beside your head. Or a cottonmouth biting you on the ankle when you're by yourself in the middle of the woods. Those things are—what's the right word?—tangible. You can see them and feel them and think about how to deal with them. But a lightning bolt, right out of the clear blue sky?"

"It won't clear. It were a damn thunder storm. And night, not blue."

"You know what the fuck I meant." Mingo picked up a plastic Burger King cup from the table and sipped through the straw.

"Want a drop more of vodka in there?" Shaky asked.

"No use. I can't taste it noway. Maybe I should quit drinking. I just feel like that lightning bolt meant something, like my life ain't what it's supposed to be. Like it's incomplete." Mingo watched Shaky mash a green pea between his fingers. "You don't have any idea what I'm talking about do you?"

"I don't think you do neither. Say, I believe I might run over to Best Buy and look at them TVs."

"You ain't got any money to buy a TV."

"Don't plan to," Shaky said. "I just like watching them all turned on at the same time. They all showing the same show but all a little bit different from the one another, and the sounds from the same shows all coming to you at different times. That's 'cause sounds travels. It's like some kind of, I don't know, some kind of dream. Sometimes it feels to me like everything's just a big dream."

"I wish like hell it was." Mingo changed the television channel. A bald man with a wide, red face in a suit was speaking into the camera.

"I will strike like lightning, thus saith the Lord! Brothers and sisters, the wrath of God is about to fall upon us like a bolt from the sky unless we join the revolution of righteousness! Are you ready to join the Almighty's mighty militia?"

"You gonna turn that?" Shaky asked.

"Shut the fuck up!"

Mingo watched the rest of the minister's sermon. At the end, Mingo wrote down the web address. "Hand me my phone."

Shaky got the cell phone from the far end of the table and gave it to Mingo.

"Goddamnit," Mingo said. "No reception." He swung his legs off the side of the bed.

"You better wait," Shaky said. "What about them tubes and shit?"

Mingo removed the IV from the back of his hand and the electrodes from his chest and left the room as Shaky followed. Just before Mingo reached the nurses' station he got online service. He typed in the web address he had seen on television. When the webpage appeared he tapped the "Contact Our Ministries" button. He entered his name and email address and wrote: *I know you were talking right to me today. I know the Lord strikes like lightning because he hit me. Tell me what to do now.*

"Since you up, let's go back and get that boat. Haaayah," Shaky said.

"Shut the fuck up."

FEBRUARY, 2018

At 6:00 AM Blevins called Tom and asked for his bank account number.

"Whatever for?" Tom asked.

"I'm transferring all my savings into it."

"The Libertad de Cuba Banco will be happy about that. Does this mean you're coming down here?"

"I'll explain everything later."

Blevins was waiting at the door when his bank opened. He took ten thousand dollars in cash and instructed a reluctant vice president to transfer his savings and annuities, despite early withdrawal penalties, into Tom's account. He then went to United Mutual where he did the same with all of his investments.

He drove to the Forest.

As Blevins stepped from the truck, Mingo stormed out of the front door of his house.

"Leave my property, Bombardi."

"Where is she?"

"Where's who?"

Blevins pointed his .45 at Mingo. "Don't fuck with me, Mingo. I'm not leaving without her."

Mingo took a chewing tobacco bag from his pocket and placed a wad in his mouth. "Looks like you might be waiting a long time. She left with some of them Starlights last night. They was getting away from the hurricane. See them clouds building over yonder? But didn't tell me where they was headed to."

A gust of wind blew dust into Blevins's face. "You're a liar."

"No need for you to get ugly about it. If you go trailing after them, you just might catch up to her."

Blevins cocked the hammer on the pistol.

"In cold blood, Bombardi? I'm not your wife, you know."

The impact was on Blevins's left temple. I saw a flash, as if a lightning bolt exploded inside of his head, and he fell to the ground. The dirt scraped his right cheek. He raised his head a few inches to see two Mingos. His ears rang, and nausea washed through him.

Someone rolled him onto his back and sat on his chest. He felt something cool and sharp press against his neck just under his larynx. He blinked and tried to focus his vision. Slowly, Diana's face came together.

"You killed my Mother."

"Yes."

"You killed her on purpose."

"Yes."

"You knew about the affair."

"Yes."

"I should cut your throat now."

"Yes."

"Do it!" Mingo yelled.

"Do it," Blevins said.

A dog barked. Diana turned her head.

I could move now, Blevins thought.

"What the fuck?" Mingo said, and Diana was knocked off of Blevins. Blevins could hear Diana and someone else struggling as he tried to stand but was dizzy and pitched onto his face. He looked around for his gun. He saw Mingo's boots scramble by him, heard a thud and a grunt and Diana saying something, and when he arose to his knees, he saw Mingo standing with his left arm curled under Diana's arm and across her chest. His hand covered her mouth and pulled her face to the side. His right hand held the knife to her neck. The sling dangled from Diana's hand. Purvis Driggers sat on the ground holding his jaw and panting.

"She ain't her but looking like Martha so much," Purvis said. "I shitted my pants again and the big man going to hurt her what ain't Martha."

Shaky was on the porch, wide-eyed and pacing. The squirrely dog barked.

"Now this is some kind of sight, ain't it, Bombardi," Mingo

said. "Whoever that son of a bitch is just gave you salvation, at least for a minute or two. Now what should I do here?"

Blevins saw his pistol under Mingo's left boot.

"Here's a good start," Mingo said. He twisted Diana around and kissed her on the mouth. She struggled, but her arms were pinned against Mingo's chest. She raised her foot and slammed it down hard against Mingo's left shin.

"Bitch!" Mingo bellowed. He lifted his leg and shoved Diana to the ground.

Blevins lunged for the pistol.

He heard two gunshots.

Mingo dropped to his knees. He reached up and pressed a hand to his chest.

Blevins rolled over and saw Moreno on one knee, still pointing her pistol at Mingo.

"Big man been shotted," Purvis said.

"Struck like lightning," Mingo said.

Blevins pushed Diana onto her stomach and reached for the handcuffs in his back pocket. She squirmed and elbowed him in the stomach.

Purvis crawled over and clutched Diana's legs. "You be being still now." She kicked him in the face but he held fast.

Blevins got the cuffs on Diana and pulled her up to her knees. He took the sling from her hand and stuffed it into his pocket. The dog leaped from the porch and charged at them. Blevins point his revolver at the dog.

"No!" Diana screamed.

The dog licked Diana's face.

Mingo lurched backwards and leaned on an elbow. Blood covered the front of his overalls. "I walk through the valley of the shadow of death. My God is an angry . . ." He slipped onto his back, his eyes open as if admiring a clear blue sky.

Shaky sat on the lip of the porch, sobbing. "I ain't got no damn body now. Even my dog done forsaken me. Haaawah."

"Big man dead," Purvis said. "I been following you the sheriff but this girl what ain't the real Martha."

Blevins looked around at Moreno, who was on both knees, vomiting.

"What are you doing here?" Blevins asked.

Moreno spat and wiped her mouth with the hand that held the pistol. "Sheriff Todd. He told me to keep an eye on you." She heaved but did not puke again. "Said to call in if you did something suspicious." She sat back on her heels, turned her face up, and inhaled deeply.

"Did you call in?"

"Not yet."

Blevins squatted. "Here's what you tell them. I called you and told you that Driggers confessed to me to killing the cryptozoologist and the bears and monkeys and that he was out here with Mauser. When you got here to arrest Driggers, a squabble ensued. Mauser came at you with a knife, so you shot him. Double tap, just like you've been trained."

"Why Driggers?"

"Just tell them that's what I told you. They'll figure out in time it wasn't him. This'll give me some time."

"Time?"

"I'll explain it all some day."

"Say what I did?" Purvis said. "Thus some kind of hand job dance I'm in. Wait. Look." He reached to the ground and picked up a ball bearing. "Look it the marble I founded."

"Here, Purvis," Blevins said. "Take this." He handed the sling to Purvis.

"Thanks you." Purvis stood and put the ball bearing into the sling's pouch. He rocked it like a pendulum and smiled.

"Sir," Moreno said. "I don't understand. Shouldn't I just report what happened?"

"There's far more going on here than you know, than you should know."

Diana yanked at her cuffs. "Let me go!"

"Quiet, Diana," Blevins said. "Moreno, just believe me. This is what is best for everyone."

"They're going to ask you a whole lot of questions."

"No they won't. I'm leaving right now."

"I'm confused by all of this."

Blevins stroked Diana's black hair. "I know. Just say what I told you, and it'll all take care of itself. Radio the department and get some people out here. Cuff Driggers."

"What about the guy on the porch?" Moreno asked. She lifted Purvis to his feet and cuffed his hands behind his back.

"He won't be any trouble. Soon as we look the other way he'll probably run off, which is for the best, too. Now I'm leaving. You won't see me again. Roberta, you're going to make a fine law enforcement officer."

Blevins led Diana toward the truck. Moreno followed.

"Blevins," Moreno said, "that's the girl in the picture, right?"

Blevins put Diana into the back seat. He left the cuffs on her and secured the safety belt.

"The dog," Diana said. "I want the dog."

"Shaky?" Blevins called. "Can we have your dog?"

Shaky was sitting by Mingo. "If I give her to you, will y'all leave me alone? I promise I won't say nothing, and God knows I don't need to do no more time."

"Deal," Blevins said.

"Her name's Phoebe. Just call her."

"Phoebe," Blevins said. "Here Phoebe." The dog looked at Blevins and cocked her head.

"Phoebe!" Diana called. The dog ran and jumped into the truck beside Diana.

Blevins climbed in behind the wheel. He looked towards the house to see Purvis turn sideways and wave with his cuffed hands. The clouds moved, and some sunlight struck Purvis's face. He broke into a broad grin, like a man proud of a well executed task.

★ ★ ★ ★ ★ ★ ★ ★ ★ ★ ★ ★ ★ ★

The radio station meteorologist announced that Hurricane Artemis had been upgraded to a category five storm with winds at 175 miles per hour. She was expected to make landfall at Titusville around 7:00 PM and continue towards Ocala at about twenty miles per hour.

"Where are you taking me?" Diana asked.

"Cedar Key."

"What for?"

"To get my boat."

Diana kicked the back of the seat. "Then what?"

"Cuba. Going to see your Uncle Tom and Aunt Martha."

"Jesus Christ. You think we're just going to be one big happy family?"

Blevins swallowed a pill. "It'll take time."

"There's a fucking hurricane coming, you know?"

"We'll be far down the coast by the time it crosses the state. You know, Cuba has some good schools. Veterinary school."

"What are the guys at the marina going to think when they see you with a girl in handcuffs? I'll tell them you're a sex trafficker."

"They know who I am, and they mind their own business."

"You can't get away with this shit. They'll find you in Cuba."

"Doesn't matter. Even if they try to charge me with something, we don't have an extradition agreement with Cuba. They can't touch me." Blevins looked at Diana in the rearview mirror. She had changed so much in only two years: the long hair, thin cheeks, a slight notch of a scar at the corner of her mouth right where her finger tips would touch as she drew back her bow. "How did you get mixed up with that Pyron guy?"

"I'm not mixed up with anything. I do as I please."

"And it pleases you to kill bears and monkeys, not to mention a camper?"

"Does it please you that I learned it all from you?"

Blevins reached under the seat for his bottle of bourbon and had a swallow. "You know you could have killed me with that sling."

"Yes, if I'd wanted to," Diana said.

"Or with the arrow that you sank into that tree by my head. Why didn't you kill me when you had the chance?"

"I needed to ask you about Mama."

"Why wait for me at Mauser's?"

"He was supposed to help me with it. Give me some of that."

He turned half way around and held the bottle to her lips and tried to watch the road. She leaned forward and drank. She pulled away, spilling a few drops onto her tank top.

"About Mauser," he said. "What were you doing with him?"

"Another drink."

Blevins held the bottle for her again. She took a longer pull this time.

"Reverend Pyron put me in contact, said Mingo would look after me. When the Reverend was killed, things fell apart. The church people started blaming each other and were fighting among themselves and some other Pyron people. I think Mingo wanted to kill them all, said they'd fucked up the apocalypse."

"Diana," Blevins said, "do you really believe all that apocalyptic stuff?"

"Do you really believe this is going to work out between us?"

"Darling, I'm not losing you again."

"You'd have to have me back to lose me again."

"We'll get you a dog."

"I already have one right here."

"Well, another one then."

"Airedale."

At the marina, Blevins signed his truck over to the dock master and gave him a thousand dollars in cash. The wind in the Gulf was at twenty knots, and the sea was choppy as the Diana II pulled out of Cedar Key. Havana was almost directly south about 420 miles or about 365 nautical miles, yet Cuba seemed closer to Blevins than the girl standing at the bow, hugging Phoebe, swaying in time with the swells of the sea, and Blevins wondered what the dog dancer heard from the fyce at her chest. Diana's blue-black hair streamed behind her. Every now and then water sprayed over the rail and onto her face. She turned to starboard, and maybe it was the scar, but Blevins thought he saw the corner of her mouth turned up in a smile. He knew it was probably wishful thinking, something he had not known for a long time.

THE END